Seashells & Mistletoe

First Edition.

Designed by Lictoria Art.

Character art by Lictoria Art.

Edited by Kayla Morton.

ISBN 979-8-89814-505-7

ISBN ebook 979-8-89814-508-8

Seashells & Mistletoe

KAY LEYDA

For Christopher, who brings me peppermint mochas and gives me mistletoe kisses. You are my forever favorite Christmas present. Thank you for four years of love and support on this wild journey. I write the stories I've imagined of all my life because you make it possible to pursue my dreams.

Both Feet on Solid Ground, Little Elf

NORTH

Another day passed like molasses dripping from a spoon as North Snowstorm wrapped perfectly presentable presents. Christmas would arrive in just over a month, so things at the North Pole were about as hectic as could be expected. At one hundred and thirteen years old, North was considered a young adult by Christmas elf standards.

He had spent every day of his life thus far in the village of the North Pole. A dutiful son, North had followed his father into gift wrapping. They had a knack for it, his dad liked to say, it was practically in their blood. The Snowstorms had been gift wrappers for six generations.

While he could practically wrap the perfect present with his eyes closed, North found himself bored to tears as yet another day crawled by. Every ribbon curled to perfection, every corner sharp and crisp. The pile of empty wrapping paper rolls beside him grew as the stack of gifts materialized in front of him.

Blue eyes snagged on the item he had just picked up—it was a snowglobe Port Townsend, Washington, according to the plaque on the front. In it, a white washed lighthouse sat at the edge of a cliff, above the blue-grey sea. When North shook it, the smallest snowflakes floated around like a snow flurry.

Wonder overtook him as he watched the glittering bits settle back down on the frozen waves. A world so different from everything he knew existed there—humans, cars, corporate jobs. North had always had a fascination with the human world and their changing seasons. He longed to feel the summer sun on his face, the cool breeze from the sea instead of the chilly wind of the Arctic.

His mind remained preoccupied as he wrapped the last dozen or so presents on his docket for the day. In his daydreams, North sat at a cafe beside the sea. Staring out at the rolling waves, the sandy beach, the shining sun. Soaking up the sounds of life in a bustling town like Port Townsend, full of people hurrying to their jobs and then home to their families.

What would it be like, to live a life like that? To be able to travel freely and see the world, to meet new people and experience life outside the confining border of his little village. He ran one hand through his blonde hair, ruffling it as he closed his eyes and tried to imagine himself there.

Could there be a job waiting for him out there in the wide, wide world? One that he would enjoy, that he would get up every day excited to do? The idea seemed absolutely ridiculous and North knew that if he told anyone what he was thinking, they would laugh at him.

Christmas elves didn't leave the North Pole. They didn't

visit human cities and they didn't work or live outside of this village, where all his family and friends were content to stay forever. He had never met anyone who felt as he did; the longing for a life he had never known, the magic of possibilities. He sighed dejectedly.

"Well, then, what's the matter there, Northy boy?" a loud voice startled him from his thoughts just as a warm hand clamped down on his shoulder.

His father, Glacier Snowstorm, stood before him. At five feet and four inches, he was nearly the tallest elf in the history of Christmas elves. Only North and his brother, West, were taller. A point of pride for the Snowstorm family, much like their generations of gift wrappers.

"Oh, it's nothing, Papa," North hurried to reply.

"Let's get on home then, my boy!" The older elf clapped him on the back. "I'm sure your Mama has something delicious waiting for us."

The two blonde haired elves headed toward the exit of Gift Wrapping Central, the second largest building in their village. As they walked, a third blonde-haired man materialized beside them. North's older brother, West, had icy blue eyes and hair that was so blonde it was practically white.

Also a gift wrapper by trade, West was fifteen years older than North. He had been settled into his role by the time his younger brother had been deemed responsible enough to begin working. Supervising North's first year at Gift Wrapping Central had fallen to his older brother, and the two had gotten into a rhythm.

A gentle thwack on the back of his head made West turn to the other elf. He raised one blonde eyebrow and made a face at his brother.

"You're daydreaming again, snowflake," whispered West.

"It's nothing," North replied quickly, glancing at their father's back. "Don't worry about it."

The three elves entered their cozy little cottage with boisterous laughter. Warm rugs and enticing smells greeted them. His eyes swept the room, finding his mother at the hearth. She stirred a cauldron over a roaring fire, soot in her hair and smudged on her cheek. West picked her up in a bear hug and spun her around.

Mama giggled as he set her down again, her feet safely on the ground.

"There are my darling boys!" She chuckled.

"What's for dinner, Mama?" asked their father.

"Barley stew and fresh caught salmon," she replied.

Moments later, the four of them settled into their designated seats at the dining table. Mama and Papa sat opposite each other, with the boys between them. North loved this time of day the best—the whole family, home together, sharing a warm meal. They traded stories about their day, as they always did over dinner.

But in the corner of his mind, North could still see the lighthouse surrounded by snowflakes in the snowglobe. His heart yearned for the new sights and sounds, something other than the perfectly predictable monotony of his cozy little life in the North Pole.

Underneath the table, West kicked him in the shin. He yelped, then quickly looked away, pretending to yawn. When Mama turned back to her bowl, he tossed a frustrated look at his older brother.

"What?" he mouthed, rubbing his shin.

"Both feet on solid ground, little elf," whispered West.

North rolled his eyes. His brother always seemed to know when his mind wandered off to the great, wide world beyond their little corner of the Arctic. Now that he was full grown and earning his own keep, he found it a bit patronizing. Did West never wonder about the world beyond their little village?

He wished even a single other Christmas elf had ever expressed the kind of longing that he felt all of the time. It seemed everyone here was perfectly content with the map laid out for them. North didn't begrudge them their happiness—he only wished to find his own.

These Contaminated Waters

CASCADIA

Deep beneath the rolling waves of the surface, Cascadia swam through frigid waters, her tail strong and steady. The chill surrounded her completely, not quite solid as ice but something nearing it. In her gills, she could feel the freezing water trying to crystalize. That night, the sea would surely freeze over.

But for now, in the wan light of a winter's day, the selkie moved fluidly through the grey-blue sea. A thick layer of blubber protected her against the low temperatures, her dark hair wild as she hurtled through the currents. For Cascadia, this was joy.

A wail sounded from behind her, mournful and high pitched. Her sisters, Nerissa and Ellery, raced after her. They knew they would not catch her—Cascadia was the fastest selkie to grace their pod in two generations. Her deep brown eyes scanned the open waters ahead of them, ensuring no large sea creature blocked their path.

Out here, so far from the shore, the humans and their boats rarely ventured during this part of the year. Cascadia understood that when the sea froze, sealing her kind beneath its icy surface, so too did the land freeze. The humans lacked any fur or blubber to protect themselves from the cold, so they hid inside their walls of stone.

She thought it a shame that they should miss the beauty the sea had to offer during these cold, dark months. To be so fragile that they could not plunge beneath the waves and swim beside the stingrays, to touch the coral with their own hands. Such things brought her unspeakable happiness.

Cascadia careened toward the east, out into the open waters of the deep. Up ahead, she knew, lay a kelp forest that would allow her to play at hiding. It was one of their favorite games. And Ellery would cheer up quickly, as she hid better than any of them amongst the waving green stalks. That would improve everyone's mood in turn.

Suddenly, a massive shadow blocked out the watery sunlight filtering down through the waves. She rolled onto her back, looking up with dark eyes at the ship that crossed her path. Above her, the dark hull of the man-made creature lingered. Entirely too close for her comfort.

"Dive, sisters," Cascadia warbled. "Out of sight."

The three chubby, furred bodies shot toward the sea floor. Dark hair streamed behind them as they pushed themselves faster, faster. Their powerful tails pushed them further from the shadow of that threat. Nothing good came of getting too close to a human ship.

When the waves crashed and the wind bit with an icy chill, only the bravest or stupidest of humans ventured out to sea. They had lost two cousins in the last five moons to such incidents. Selkies who had ventured a bit closer than necessary to the human boats, just a little too far from the rest of the pod.

Those selkies had disappeared, never to be seen again. There were stories told by the old ones, by Cascadia's mother's mother, of selkies who had wished to see the land and all it had to offer. To do so meant to shed their selkie furs, hidden among fallen logs and rocks, and take the form of humans. Two legs where their tails had been.

For most, they had spent merely a day or two among the strange creatures above the sea's surface. Returned with stories of human men with selfish hearts and rough hands, who had wanted to keep them. Selkies who enjoyed the kisses of those men but refused to let go of their hearts, and dove back into the sea.

A few, though, in recent memory had come home moons later, even whole sun-seasons after they had left the depths. They spoke of life on land as if it were just as real, just as much a part of them, as the lives they lived beneath the waters. Of leaving behind a life, a family, on those distant shores.

Of children they had borne, more human than seal. Who breathed the air of the surface and could not survive in the cold depths of the ocean. Children who could not come with them when they returned to their home beneath the waves. Those selkies mourned for the rest of their tides, heartbroken at having to leave them behind.

Cascadia knew the risks. She knew all that the land and humans could take from her, if she was not careful. But she would be twenty suns next tide, and she had the same right as every ancestor to take her day of exploration.

The old ones had become more insistent, of late, that the younger selkies stop their tradition. They said it was no longer safe, the way it had been in their youth, and their old ones' youth. Humans were changing, their world was changing.

As the number of land-dwellers multiplied, the oceans became more unstable. Waste and sludge found their way into the water at a frightening speed, polluting their seas and killing the creatures that lived there. Whole species had disappeared, fished to extinction and bred in captivity to feed the humans.

Surely if Cascadia could go to land herself, if she could see what they were doing and find out why, she could do something about it. If someone did not do something soon, the sea would not be habitable for much longer. Her sisters worried about bringing selkings into these contaminated waters. More and more were born with deformities.

Her pod had taken up residence in a series of sea caves far out from the shores of the nearest human lands. They enjoyed all the wild sea had to offer. But the hunters and the fishers were exploring further and further out with each passing sun. How much longer could her kind hide beneath the waves?

There were no answers to be found here, in the coves and kelp forests of her youth. A pod of nearly four dozen sought the kind of carefree life their old ones told tales of, the world of long ago when land-dwellers had only ships carved of trees and powered by their own arms.

Given the chance, Cascadia would find out what she

could about the world above. She would see if there was anything she could do to help her pod survive what was to come. The selkie steeled her gaze as she glanced back over her shoulder at the shadow of a ship far above, her dark eyes full of determination.

Adventure Awaits

NORTH

November 25th was the day after tomorrow. Exactly one month until Christmas. The whole village was in a tizzy, following their schedule to the minute. If everything went according to plan, then all would be well. It was all North's parents or coworkers discussed. Staying the course; another flawless Christmas.

He couldn't stand it. The thought bored him to tears. He could only fake a cough and look away to hide the rolling of his eyes so many times before someone sent him to the infirmary. Elves would assume he had come down with something, from the way North covered his mouth with his fist and cleared his throat for the eightieth time.

Then an idea struck him. While elves didn't celebrate Christmas to the extent that humans did, they had adopted many of the human customs surrounding the holiday. If North could work up the courage, perhaps he could ask for a Christmas present of his own. The moment his lunch break began, he took off like a rabbit.

Stately and imposing, the Claus's estate at the edge of the village looked every bit as regal as it should. Red brick stacked layer over layer, towering to three floors, a flat roof that doubled as the landing pad for the eight reindeer. Snow covered the building in drifts and piles, partially melted from the midday sun. It would freeze back over come sundown, when the temperature would drop significantly.

North summoned every ounce of bravery he possessed, then raised his hand and knocked. The sound reverberated for a moment, then fell away. A few tense moments of absolute silence followed and he genuinely considered turning away. But then the heavy wooden door swung open and Santa's butler arched one fluffy eyebrow.

"Can I help you, lad?"

"Yes, sir," shouted North, then cleared his throat and spoke more softly. "I wish to speak with the Big Man, if he is not too busy at the moment."

"Not too busy?" scoffed the other elf, shaking his head.

"I understand if he's not available, given the circumstances, of course," North continued quickly.

"Humph!" cried the well-dressed elf. "Wait here."

An interminable time passed as he waited in the foyer, self-conscious of the snow melting off his boots and onto the elegant entryway rug. His blue eyes took in every detail of the hallway—the pristine white walls, the heavy picture frames holding photos of Santa and Mrs. Claus over the years, the carpeted stairs leading up to their personal quarters. It really stood out against the elfish cottages North was used to.

The sound of footsteps echoed down the hall as the

butler made his way back to the entryway. Though he scowled a bit, he nodded.

"Santa will see you."

"Oh, wow, really?" gasped North, running a hand through his blonde hair.

"Yes. Now don't keep him waiting, boy," snapped the other elf.

That was how North Snowstorm found himself before the one and only Santa Clause. Or so he thought, until the big chair spun to reveal Mrs. Claus instead. Her rosy cheeks and soft smile were full of kindness. The wisps of white hair that had slipped from her chignon framed her face in a way that complimented her quite well.

But this had not been what he expected and North was incredibly confused.

"H-Hello there! Good afternoon, Mrs. Claus," he stammered.

"Good afternoon to you, young Snowstorm," replied the grandmotherly woman. "What is it you have come to ask?"

He blinked at her for several seconds, completely derailed from his previously practiced words for Santa. Eyes like sapphires, she watched him.

"Oh, right, yes. Well then," North managed to choke out, straightening to his full height.

"I admit, I had expected you days ago." Mrs. Claus winked.

"W-what?!" he gasped. "You were...expecting me? I don't understand."

"Go on, then, youngster. Make your request."

North cleared his throat again, feeling silly. "Well,

ma'am, I was wondering...if it would be possible for me to make a Christmas wish this year."

"What a clever elf you are!" She clapped her hands together. "I will consider it. Please tell me exactly what it is you'd wish for."

"I want to see the human world," he blurted out.

"Can you be more specific?" Mrs. Claus asked patiently.

"I wish to spend the next thirty days among the humans, to see Christmas as they see it," North explained as best he could. "I want to see the world beyond our icy realm. I'm terribly sorry if that sounds ungrateful, after all that you have given us."

Her soft chuckle caused him to glance back up at her. "Not at all, young Snowstorm. It has been an age since one of ours dared to do such a thing."

"I'm...not the first?" he blinked in surprise.

"Oh, no, young elf," Mrs. Claus smiled indulgently. "Our own boy, Nicholas, was the last to request such an adventure of his own, many years ago now."

"I had no idea," murmured North.

The sound of a bell jingling interrupted his thoughts. He realized that Mrs. Claus had pressed a button to get someone's attention. The pitter-patter of little feet sounded in the hall just before the door to the office opened behind him.

"You rang, Missus?" chimed a sweet voice.

A voice he recognized. The prettiest elf in his class, Juniper Snowdrop, stood beside him now. Her blonde curls were perfectly pulled back with a green velvet bow, matched to the green velvet dress she wore. Her bright eyes met his briefly before she returned her focus to the mistress of the house.

"Our young Snowstorm will be needing some things," Mrs. Claus informed her. "Will you gather what he requires for a trip to the world outside?"

"The world outside?" Juniper gasped.

The lady of the house nodded, smiling at him. "Indeed. Adventure awaits!"

"Yes, Mrs. Claus," the elf bowed, scurrying from the room.

"You will have one month to experience the world south of here. Then you will come home and resume your duties, unless something more important arises," she informed him.

North agreed without hesitation. It was exactly what he had asked for, and more than he had hoped to get, in all honesty. He wondered if Santa himself would have offered him the same deal, or if this was a special kindness from Lady Christmas. Rumors had said she had a heart of generosity and a weakness for love stories.

He would have his chance to test that theory, then. Mrs. Claus told him to go home and spend one last night with his family, to say his goodbyes properly. And then return to her here the morning of November 25th, before the sun rose. Heart thundering in his chest, North walked back the way he had come.

Running both hands through his messy blonde locks, he steeled himself for the argument with his parents. He wanted this opportunity more than he had ever wanted anything in his life, but they would not understand. North hated the idea that they would think he despised his life here, with his family.

But the curiosity, the tug toward the world beyond their

icy village, had been pulling at him more forcefully in the last few years. It was undeniable to him now.

Hunting a Seal

CASCADIA

Fear coursed through Cascadia as the selkie pushed herself to her limit. Somewhere up ahead, her sister was tangled in a fishing net. If she wriggled too much, it would draw the attention of the fishermen on the boat, and they would haul up their catch. Nerissa had raced to find their pod, her wail piercing and desperate.

When she had enough information to proceed, the two had turned on their fins and taken off. It took only a few breaths for Cascadia to outpace her sister, her powerful tail straining to go faster, faster, faster. Ellery could remain calm for a short while. Not long, though. Not with the panic of capture beating in her chest.

"Sister!" Cascadia shouted, her wail plaintive. "I am here! Be still."

An answering cry reached her from a short distance away. Then Ellery was in her sights, nearly in her reach, sobbing with fear. Pulling herself to a stop just before reaching the other selkie, Cascadia held up both hands to placate her sister.

It seemed to take Ellery a considerable amount of effort to not throw herself into her sister's arms. Nerissa careened to a halt behind them, rolling over several times in her haste to stop.

"Focus, Ellery," she murmured, taking her face in both hands.

"We will get you out of that—that thing!" cried Nerissa.

"Please, Cascadia," wailed Ellery in a wavering voice. "Don't let them take me."

From her years of experience with such incidents, the selkie knew that their time would run out shortly. Those who thrashed in an attempt to free themselves from the netting only succeeded in alerting the humans above to their large catch. They knew, by now, that the fishermen hoped for a small shark, something they could sell for its meat.

Selkies, however, were a rare treasure. They were never tossed back into the water. Being captured by the land dwellers was as good as a death sentence for her kind. And Cascadia could not allow that to happen to any more of her pod. She would do anything to protect her younger sister from that fate.

"Listen to me." She locked eyes with Ellery.

When the other selkie nodded carefully, lips pressed in a tight line, she continued.

"We need something sharp to break the net," Cascadia said. "I have only this tigershark tooth—it will take a long time and a lot of sawing for it to cut you free."

"Surely it will be enough," Nerissa whined.

"Only if we can offset the weight so they do not realize what we are doing," she replied.

"How do we do that?" Ellery's wail broke her heart.

Taking a look at the sea around them, Cascadia searched for an answer. Perhaps a shark would cause enough of a distraction. She knew how to draw them from the nearby area. One hand held the massive tooth in an iron grip, the other lay palm up as she slashed roughly at the meaty flesh of her thumb.

Sure enough, blood the color of the night sky bubbled up along her skin. It would not take long for the sharks in these waters to scent her, to assume an easy kill could be found.

"Nerissa," she snapped, thrusting the tooth into her hands. "You must wait until the shark is after me, then cut her free as fast as you can."

"M-me?" gasped her sister.

"I am the fastest. I have to be the one to lead it away," Cascadia said bluntly.

"There are two places where my tail is tangled," Ellery whined. "How will your shark distract the humans from the second pull on their net?"

Her dark eyes met Ellery's, then Nerissa's in turn. "I will lead the shark close enough to the surface to distract the land dwellers. They will likely assume another is trying to get at their catch."

"Are you sure this will work?" whined Nerissa, concern written on her face.

"It is our best option in this moment," Cascadia advised them.

Scanning the seas in all directions, she kept her eyes

wide as she sought out the creature that would facilitate their daring escape. There! A juvenile hammerhead swam lazily in their direction, turning his head slowly from side to side.

Once he spotted them, she would have moments to draw his attention away from her sisters. But if she could get closer, block his view of Ellery and Nerissa, then she could guarantee that he would follow her. A blubbery, round selkie made for a very promising meal for the likes of him.

"Wait until he sees me, then hurry!" Cascadia told her sisters.

Then she took off in the direction of the hammerhead, squeezing the cut on her hand to draw more of her blue blood to the surface. Her plan worked like a charm; one black eye narrowed in on her and then the shark began to move with purpose. Slowly, as if she were injured, she backed away from him.

A careful dance followed—the shark had crossed paths with selkies before, Cascadia could tell from the way he hesitated before following her. He did not rush her the way he would with smaller prey. As if he knew that this type of creature could be tricky, less helpless than she appeared.

Cascadia prayed to the stars above that it would fall for her ruse. Her sister's life depended on it. Heart beating wildly in her ribcage, she let the shark get closer than she would under any other circumstances. He struggled to keep her in his gaze, with those split eyes on either side of his head.

"Now!" she wailed as loudly as she could, shooting off toward the surface.

Behind her, the shark picked up his pace. She could feel

the water change, see the way all the fishes and smaller creatures darted out of the way. It was not her they feared, but him. The hammerhead's razor sharp teeth could kill them in a single bite.

Though they were the easier prey, Cascadia knew that this shark had his sights set on her. A meal of this size would feed him for many tides, or feed a family. Perhaps he did not travel alone. That would bode very badly for her. Still, she threaded through the waves at half speed, letting him gain a bit of distance on her.

With a deep pull of sea water into her gills, Cascadia threw herself out of the water. The fishing boat floated just a few paces away, a handful of humans on the deck in their brightly colored gear. Easy to spot, even on a dreary day such as this. Sunlight glittered off the water droplets as she arced through the air, suddenly heavy in a way that surprised her.

She wailed again, mimicking the sound of an injured seal. Then she hit the water and plunged back into its depths, cold and deep and refreshing. Disoriented, Cascadia blinked her dark eyes several times to regain her vision after the brightness of the world above. A shout sounded distantly above her.

"Shark!"

"Look, men! Hurry!"

The ship lurched to one side as the crew threw themselves against the railing, craning their necks to get a look at the grim scene. Far too close for her comfort, the hammerhead had followed her briefly above the water, and he shook the seas when he flopped back down into the waves. *How strange*, Cascadia thought.

But she had only a moment to ponder this new experience before the shark would be upon her. At top speed, she raced toward the side of the boat. Now that the land dwellers were watching, she would not risk breaching the waters again.

If she got close enough to the surface, though, they would see only her vague shape from up on their ship. And they would see the fin and tail of the shark that chased her, when he barreled after Cascadia in full pursuit. More shouting trickled to her.

"He's there!"

"He's hunting a seal!"

Again, the boat above her shifted. The humans had followed her to this side, easily able to spot the shark so close to the water's edge. If Nerissa had successfully freed Ellery, she could be done with this charade. Cascadia dove under the boat, rolling fluidly as she turned to get a glimpse of her sisters.

Sure enough, her dark eyes caught movement. The soft brown fur of her sisters as they pulled away from the fishing net, their long waves of dark hair trailing behind them. *Thank the stars*, Cascadia thought.

"Hide!" she wailed, hoping they would return to the caves their pod slept in.

When they took off in that direction, she swam rapidly another way. Leading the shark away while they made the most direct path to safety ought to buy them some time. Still, it would be difficult to lose the hammerhead.

Cascadia pushed herself to her limits, heading toward the shallow waters of a sheltered cove she knew of. The shark would not be able to follow her onto the shore. If she could just reach that rocky entrance, she could scramble over the boulders and into the shallows where he couldn't follow.

Behind her, the shark began to close the distance between them. His powerful tail, far sleeker than hers, allowed his massive form to glide through the water almost effortlessly. But the rocks were just ahead, within sight. Cascadia strained, a final burst of energy coursing through her, as she dove down.

If she timed this just right, the selkie could propel herself out of the water and over the wall of rocks, out of reach of the hammerhead who pursued her. Her heart raced as she pumped her furry tail hard once she somersaulted toward the surface. Meanwhile, the shark had stayed his course, heading right for her.

It took five heartbeats for Cascadia to leap through the emptiness above the sea. Five heartbeats from the time the crown of her head breached the water until she crashed back into the shallows on the other side. She hit the sandy shore hard, skidding to a stop with a painful roll onto her back.

The water here had not been deep enough for her to dive straight in. There existed only a single selkie's height worth of crystal blue sea above the sand covered beach she found herself sitting on now. Her deep brown eyes blinked at the unfamiliar feeling of the air around her face, the lack of sea salt in her gills.

A thundering crash shook the little cove, the waves rocking sharply against her middle as Cascadia turned back toward the open water. There, behind a few massive boulders, waited the hammerhead shark. He must have rammed straight into the rocks in hopes of dislodging them to get to her. And failed.

Safe for the moment, the selkie observed the little stretch of sand she found herself on. A few pieces of driftwood, some seashells, a few trees further back from the water's edge. Nothing out of the ordinary.

In all her moons, Cascadia had never been this close to leaving the embrace of the sea that she called home. The breeze floated past, ruffling her damp fur and making her dark hair dance. Suddenly, she could not breathe.

Furry hands scrabbled at her throat, where her gills had closed. Panic threatened to overtake her before the words of an old one came to her.

"In the world above, there is no sea to breathe. The humans breathe through their speaking hole, where they also eat."

Cascadia had never truly considered what this would mean for her trip to the land dwellers world. The need to learn how to take air into her lungs, like a human, instead of water through her gills as she had always done. But many selkies had survived the transition over all the generations before her, so it could not be too difficult to master.

Carefully, she opened her mouth as if to wail, to communicate to her sisters. She sucked in the thin, transparent air and felt her lungs inflate. Then she blew out the breath, and the buzzing in her head abated. Air. How strange it was to require air for the first time in her life.

Thank You for Everything, Lady Christmas

NORTH

As the sun rose over their little cottage, North Snowstorm packed a few of his favorite things into a knapsack to bring with him on his adventure. Dinner with his family had been miserable, just as North had expected. Mama and Papa were heartbroken, positively devastated at the news. And West...West was furious. Disappointed in him.

"I just know there's something out there waiting for me," he whispered into the quiet morning.

Into his bag went a snowglobe of their little village in the North Pole, his favorite hand-me-down bowtie from Papa, and a well-loved copy of his favorite book. *The Lion, the Witch, and the Wardrobe* by C. S. Lewis. A story of family, adventure, a frozen kingdom, and kindness triumphing over cruelty. North had longed for such an adventure for as long as he could remember.

He truly hated that he needed to choose between his family, his home, and his adventure. But all the good things in life required making difficult choices and stepping out of your comfort zone, or so his parents had always told him. They only disagreed now because it meant being away from them.

In the living room, his family waited to say their goodbyes. Mama's eyes were filled with tears and Papa's mouth wobbled like he might break down, too. Beside them, West glared at the front door, his mouth set.

"I promise to be back soon," North started, reaching for them.

"It isn't safe out there!" Mama cried.

"You know how dangerous it is for our kind," his brother grumbled. "What if someone figures out what you are? What if you get stuck and can't get home?"

North took a deep breath. "Mrs. Claus has taken care of everything. She's sending me to the same place her son went for his year abroad. There's a good community of magical creatures there. I won't be alone."

"A community of magical creatures?" Papa perked up at that.

"She's arranged a place for me to stay and people to look after me," North continued. "Please don't worry too much. I promise I'll be careful."

"How can we not worry?" Mama sniffled, wiping at her nose.

"I'll write to you every day, so that you know I'm fine," he added quickly.

Begrudgingly, they wrapped him in a hug. Unsurprisingly, Mama was the last to let go. She fidgeted with her apron and made him promise to write them every day, no exceptions. Then they stood in the front window and waved him off until North couldn't make out their cottage.

The sun rose steadily into the sky as North walked the long road back to the Claus's house. This time, the three story brick mansion felt just a tiny bit less intimidating. He had an appointment. He was expected. Mrs. Claus would be waiting for him.

He rang the bell and followed the butler up the carpeted stairs. In Santa's office, Mrs. Claus smiled brightly at him.

"Good morning, young Snowstorm!"

"G-good morning, Mrs. Claus," North managed, scratching the back of his neck.

"Are you ready for your journey?" she asked simply, those bright blue eyes sparkling in the morning sunlight.

"Yes." He nodded vigorously. "I can't ever thank you enough for this incredible opportunity. It's truly a dream come true. I still can't believe you're allowing it."

The white-haired woman held a hand up to stop his rambling and North snapped his mouth shut. She gestured to a bag standing upright near the door, little wheels on the bottom and a handle at the top.

"Everything you need is in your luggage," Mrs. Claus informed him.

North followed her up the stairs and out onto the roof. A little overhang had been built there with a comfortable couch and fluffy blankets. He could imagine Santa waiting there as the elves triple checked the reindeer's harnesses and the sleigh. But his ride appeared ready and waiting on him at that moment.

A single reindeer and the smallest sleigh he had ever seen sat in the center of the landing pad. The reindeer stamped its foot impatiently, huffing out a breath of air into the chilly morning. North stared in awe as he hurried after Mrs. Claus and the sleigh.

"Here you go, my sweet Comet." She handed the animal a large carrot. "You know what to do. Drop him off just like last time."

She handed him a little burlap bag filled with shiny red apples, advising North to feed one to the reindeer regularly throughout their journey. He nodded without hesitation. And just like that, it was time for him to go. North climbed into the little sleigh, hefting his new luggage onto the seat beside him.

His blue eyes watered as a brisk winter wind bustled across the rooftop, ruffling his hair and nearly stealing away his knitted cap. Mama would be furious if he lost it, so North grabbed at it with both hands and tucked it under his ears.

The soft blue wool with its snowflake pattern had been a Christmas present from his parents last year. It had quickly become a favorite of his, knowing Mama had stitched every line by hand and infused it with her love. West had a matching knitted cap and they often made a point of wearing them together to make Mama smile.

Sadness clenched his heart at the thought of not being here to do so for many weeks. North took a deep, steadying breath and turned to Mrs. Claus.

"Best of luck on your adventure, young elf!"

"Thank you for everything, Lady Christmas."

At that, Comet took to the sky. North gripped the sides of the sleigh tightly as they launched into the air, then settled. Even though he had grown up in the North Pole, surrounded by the reindeer and Santa's magic, it had never occurred to him to ask how the sleigh managed to stay afloat. It hadn't mattered before.

He also had no idea how long it would take to get to wherever they were going by flying reindeer. Mrs. Claus had not told him which continent she was sending him to, let alone anything more specific. North settled in for what he assumed would be a long ride with the brisk winter wind biting at his cheeks.

At first, there had been nothing to see but the snowy white of the North Pole stretching on endlessly in every direction. Then the open ocean had come into view, and North had gasped at the sight. The water's clear, shimmering surface revealed creatures he had only read about until then.

Orcas danced beneath the waves, surging and retreating as they chased each other through the ocean. They disappeared from time to time under ice floes and small islands dusted in snow, reappearing swiftly on the other side with their graceful, sleek bodies. Blonde wisps fell into North's face as he leaned over the side of the sleigh to get a better look at them.

The reindeer, Comet, drew closer to the water as if sensing his interest in the sea creatures. From this vantage point, he could see for ages down into the deep blue of the water. Fish of more kinds than he could count, and certainly more than he had ever crossed paths with in his frozen homeland, darted by in schools.

His bright blue eyes caught movement off to his left. A humpback whale breached the surface, shooting up into the air beside North, his massive flippers spread wide. When the whale flopped back into the sea, the spray of saltwater hit North square in the face.

A surprised laugh tumbled out of him at the unexpected encounter. What a story this would be to tell his family when he got home. North could imagine the look on his mother's face, the teasing from his brother, when he told them about this.

Wide awake after his unexpected bath, North ran his hands through his blonde hair and brushed it out of his face. The water had been refreshingly cold, a shock to his system. Ahead of him, the endless ocean gave way to a town of brightly colored buildings in the midst of a snowy valley.

Against the edge of the water sat a village scattered over uneven hills and surrounded by towering mountains covered in snow. North reached for his bag, assuming this must be their destination. But the reindeer never slowed down. The pretty town with its sled dogs noisy, excited barks disappeared behind them in minutes.

On they flew, Comet pulling his little sleigh through the chilly skies effortlessly. The small bag of shiny red apples that Mrs. Claus had given him for the reindeer suddenly sprang to mind, and North pulled one out to inspect.

"Comet? Would you like an apple?"

A grunt sounded softly from the creature. He took that as an affirmation and tossed the apple toward the front of the sleigh. The entire vehicle jolted sharply down and to the right as the reindeer darted to snap up the treat and it nearly caused North to tumble out of the sleigh.

Thankfully, the sides were sturdy, and he was able to regain his balance once they settled back into their smooth path. Little floating islands and snowdrifts began to appear and Comet pulled the sleigh up, further from the water. Below, seals and sea lions dotted the floating rafts of snow.

They huddled together against the cold, dozens and dozens of them on the larger islands.

North couldn't help but think of how cozy and warm he would be at home on the couch with his family, snuggled up like those seals. He could practically smell the logs burning in the fireplace, feel his mother's head resting on his shoulder.

Home was an ember of warmth and happiness, burning in his heart as he set out on his grand adventure. It would remain bright and steady. North looked forward to returning home to his family after his month of sightseeing and exploring the world beyond their tiny village. Everything he knew and loved would be there waiting for him when he got back.

The little snow covered islands gave way to bigger stretches of snowy forest. Evergreen trees dusted in powdered snow and a river rushed by below, water deep blue and churning. From his vantage point, North could make out the occasional wooden cabin, soft white smoke escaping the chimneys. It looked so familiar, so like his own home, that he couldn't help but smile.

Stunning mountains rose in the distance, blocking out the sun as it sank below the horizon. From time to time, North spotted perfectly clear, still lakes that looked like glass from where he sat. Comet called out in greeting a few times as they passed herds of his cousins—caribou, moose, and elk scattered across the icy forests and streams.

A few elk called back, their loud bugle-like sounds echoing out over the fields of snow. Sometimes they passed nothing but wild creatures for hour after hour; other times they flew just out of sight over cities bigger than North could imagine. Sprawling busy towns with traffic and cars and airplanes, all of which his reindeer companion avoided easily.

Then there were the endless green trees of the northern forests. His eyes grew heavy as the sky darkened to a deep shade of indigo and the lights of a town came into view. Up ahead, North could make out a lighthouse at the edge of a peninsula. It showed him the sleepy town in flashes of golden light followed by sweeping darkness.

When Comet slowed his gait and began drifting closer to the ground, North blinked in surprise. They landed on a snowy field with a jostle and a thump.

"We're here?"

The reindeer turned one dark eye to him and nodded, stamping one foot in confirmation. North needed nothing else, he tossed his bag over the side and hopped out of the sleigh, suddenly wide awake and full of energy. When Comet gestured with his head to a building on their right, the elf turned to follow his gaze.

A massive house, painted white and decorated with yards and yards of festive garlands, sat proudly at the top of a hill. The sign above the front entrance read "North Pole Bed & Breakfast," and he chuckled. A warm glow emanated from the windows, facing out toward the open sea like a beacon. North lifted his bag and took off on wobbly legs, tingling from sitting the whole day.

He stepped into the brightly lit front room, where a magnificent Christmas tree immediately demanded his full attention. It boasted popcorn garlands and orange peels and other natural decorations, all safe for animals to eat when the tree eventually wound up back outside. Just like their tree at his own house, in his little elf village up north.

"Welcome to the North Pole!" called a friendly voice. "Do you need a room?"

North turned to find a middle-aged woman with suspiciously pointy ears smiling up at him. Her glasses hung from her neck on a delicate gold chain, the frames a lovely shade of red.

"Y-yes! Mrs. Claus sent me," he started, realizing that if he were mistaken and she was not an elf, she would be thoroughly confused.

"Ah, good, good. She called ahead and set everything up for you, young Snowstorm." The woman nodded encouragingly. "We have a room ready for you and in the morning I can give you all the tips for exploring town. I'm sure you're ready to crash for the night."

North followed her up two flights of stairs to a bedroom on the third floor. A little golden plague labeled it "Unit E," and he smiled again at the little inside joke. When the proprietor opened the door and set a brass key on the bedside table, he opened his mouth. She held up one hand and explained without hesitation.

"You can call me Ms. Eve. This is your room key, which you will need to keep on you and return to my desk when you check out." The woman's eyes crinkled in a pleasant smile.

"Wonderful, thank you very much, Ms. Eve," North replied quickly. "I look forward to talking with you tomorrow."

With that, she nodded politely and tucked her hands

behind her back, heading back down to the front desk. His blue eyes widened as he took in the details of his temporary accommodations. A large bed with a quilted comforter in emerald green and fluffy white pillows took up about a third of the space.

He could see what he assumed to be the bathroom and instead stepped toward the porch. The floor-to-ceiling window screeched as if it had not been opened in some time, but eventually gave way. When North had slid it high enough to slip out onto the balcony, he hurried to close it behind him.

From here, the ocean felt close enough to touch. Deep, dark water and snow and ice danced in the night. He had longed to see the wonders of the world beyond his village, the sea and forests and lakes and things that the North Pole could not offer him. And now he found himself right there in the middle of it all, just like he had always dreamed.

A chilly breeze off the water snapped him out of his daydream. North hurried back inside, securing the window against the blustering wind before he turned on the hot water in the shower. Soon, a steamy haze filled the bathroom adjoined to his unit, and the elf reveled in the warmth.

After spending an entire day outdoors, flying through air cold enough to snow and freeze, the warm cascade of droplets coasting over his chilled skin felt like pure bliss. He scrubbed the dead skin away and washed his blonde hair, humming Christmas songs to himself as he bathed.

When he finished, North wrapped a fluffy white towel around his waist and stepped out of the shower. He ruffled his shoulder-length hair with another towel, tousling it until it could pass for dry enough. Then he pulled back the covers, tucked himself into the bed, and let sleep claim him.

Like Me

CASCADIA

The frozen land beneath her new feet felt like coral against Cascadia's sensitive flesh. Periodically, she grew dizzy and remembered that she needed to actively breathe with her human lungs. That water no longer rushed past her gills at every motion, doing that work for her. Everything up on land seemed unpleasant and painful.

One slow, stumbling step at a time, she made her way across the rocky beach. Her strange new limbs were surely defective, given how poorly they worked. If Cascadia stepped the wrong way, her legs collapsed out from under her and she found herself back on the ground.

Frustration coursed through her as she took another unexpected tumble, landing sideways and shouting in pain as her elbow hit the icy ground. Ahead of her, a stretch of trees rose on her left and some kind of funny-shaped wooden ship sat atop the sands on her other side.

It took Cascadia several tries to successfully stay upright before she could even consider which way she ought to go.

Despite the pull of the sea and her curiosity about the towering trees covered in snow, she knew heading toward the human structures would be the smartest decision.

Tugging her furry brown pelt tighter around her torso, she stumbled slowly forward. Sights and sounds from the strange ship up ahead began to take shape—a tall, round object moving in slow circles, the sound of gulls and music and children shouting. It tugged Cascadia ever closer to the human world, a glittering jewel on the sandy beach.

The closer she got to the rows of wooden planks, the more of it she could make out. Not a ship, then. Or not like one she had ever seen, in all her moons. Everything up there felt loud, and bright, and overwhelming. Cascadia leaned against a sturdy beam of wood that held the structure up.

Exhaustion pulled at her. Learning how to use her legs had taken more of a toll than she had realized. She sank to her knees. Carefully, still unsure how these odd limbs worked, she leaned back farther and farther until she landed on her bottom.

She listened to the sounds of the humans above her, up on the boards. Judging by all the different voices she could make out, there must be nearly as many land dwellers there as fish in the sea. Endless. Uncountable.

Worry surged fresh in her veins as she realized how daunting her goals truly were. For Cascadia to make any difference in the long-term health of the oceans she called home, she would need to learn how to appear human. How to behave, how to speak their languages, learn their customs.

At that moment, the entire endeavor felt daunting. A massive surge threatening to pull her out to the deepest sea, tumbling head over fins in its grasp. Cascadia tucked her knees against her chest, wrapping the warm brown fur of her pelt around as much of her body as she could to ward against the cold.

Despite the layer of ice that formed sometimes over the sea, she had never experienced a cold like this. Her selkie body was well insulated against the cool waters and her constant motion kept her from focusing on it. Here, on land, trapped in this strange new form, with no fur or blubber to protect her, she felt vulnerable.

Cascadia must have dozed off at some point, waking just as the first rays of light were cresting over the water's edge. Her first morning on land. Her back arched as she stretched her arms above her head, shaking out her achy limbs. That was when she remembered that she no longer had a tail, or her fur to keep her warm.

Stiff legs slowly unfolded as she got to her feet, the numbing cold biting at every inch of exposed skin. Cascadia did not like being human at all. Her dark brown pelt covered not nearly enough of her strange new body and the wild wind could cut between it and her flesh.

Carefully, Cascadia pulled her pelt around her torso and began the trek up the sandy hill to get a better look at the place. Pain lanced through her feet as she placed her full weight on them, a new and unpleasant experience.

But if she wanted to use her hands, she would have to let go of her warm fur, the only thing protecting her from the biting chill in the air. Cascadia struggled up the steep incline, struggling to find purchase when the sand shifted beneath her feet and slid out from under them.

Eventually, though, she managed to struggle to the top of the hill. A sign that read Seaside Boardwalk hung from a wrought-iron fence and Cascadia wondered what it meant. At the sound of voices, she sat down as gingerly as she could manage, and listened.

"Yeah, man, I'm down at the pier getting the coffee shop open this morning," said a deep voice.

It seemed to come from a towering dark-haired human wrapped in many layers of cloth. He held a small metal device to his ear, and spoke aloud as if in the middle of a conversation. When he pulled a key ring out of his pocket and unlocked the door to one of the small buildings, Cascadia watched him.

Suddenly, the room he had stepped into illuminated like a full moon, shining from within. As Cascadia watched, the human flipped switches and pressed buttons and moved in a strange sort of dance around the small space. Not quite a house, certainly not a ship, but something else. Only a handful of other land dwellers wandered about nearby, seemingly doing the same rituals in other little buildings.

Then a light flickered to life like an anglerfish, bright and insistent. OPEN. As if a signal had been given, two of the other humans hurried over to his place. They stepped in and spoke to him briefly, then waited a short while. When the dark-haired man handed them a white bottle shaped item, they each smiled warmly at each other, then headed back out into the cold.

"Nothing better than piping hot coffee on a day like this!" said one man to the other.

"Right you are, my friend," replied the other.

Their hands, tucked securely back in their little cloth covers, wrapped tightly around the cups as they walked back to their small buildings. Cascadia watched in fascination as each of them took a long sip from the tiny buckets and sighed contentedly. There must be some kind of warm food inside the unfamiliar bottles.

Carefully, she pushed herself back up onto her aching feet. Her dark hair hung in tangled waves over her shoulders and down her back and her brown eyes scanned the Boardwalk anxiously as she walked to the building with the glowing sign. It took what little strength she had left in her weary body to push open the door as she had seen the other land dwellers do.

When she tumbled into the brightly lit room, warmth wrapped around her like the sea on a sunny day. The dark-haired human behind the counter called out a greeting, then looked up and froze.

"Good morning! Welcome to Holly Jolly—" He set down the gadgets he had been fiddling with and rushed to her side. "Miss! Are you alright?"

Not sure how best to reply, Cascadia simply wrapped her arms around herself and allowed him to usher her into a booth at the back of the room. His blue eyes were kind as he hurried to gather his discarded layers, wrapping her up gently.

"You're...not from around here, are you?" asked the man softly.

She shook her head, hoping that much remained the same in all languages.

"First time on land?" He nodded toward her dark pelt, still wrapped around her middle. "We'd better get you dressed before anybody notices."

Before she knew it, a young woman appeared with a bundle in her arms. She gestured for Cascadia to follow her, and though it made her nervous, she obliged. In a smaller room, the woman closed the door behind them and held out several pieces of cloth.

Behind her, a mirror gave Cascadia a glimpse of what the humans saw: long, dark hair streaked with snow and frost, wild eyes, tan skin, and a curvaceous form she had never seen before. One hand reached to run through her dark locks, tangling in the unruly layers. Her reflection did the same, those brown eyes staring right back at her.

“Let me help you with that, dear,” said the human beside her.

Slowly, the young woman showed her how to put on each of the layers of cloth. They all had names, strange and unfamiliar things that Cascadia immediately forgot. But her body adjusted to the warmth radiating through the little building, and the cloth helped her hold onto it. When she was deemed appropriately dressed for land-dweller standards, the woman led her back into the larger room.

The dark-haired human smiled nervously, offering her one of the tiny white buckets she had seen the other humans get earlier.

“Would you like some coffee? It’ll help you warm up,” he said softly.

The young woman, with auburn hair and bright hazel eyes, gestured as she explained. “Warm. To drink. Like water, but dark. Will you try it?”

Cascadia hesitated only a moment before she tipped back the cup, the liquid spilling into her mouth too fast. She shrieked in pain and confusion, dropping it.

“Too hot? No, that’s okay, don’t worry about it," said the

woman. "Let's try something else. David, can you get me a hot chocolate? Room temperature, please."

Away went the land dweller, back to his noisy machines and gadgets. The young woman sat down across from her and smiled. Cascadia did her best to return the gesture.

"I'm sorry about that. It's his first encounter with your kind and he's a bit nervous," she explained.

Cascadia nodded, unsure what else to do.

"I'm Emmy and that's David. I've lived here all my life and know lots about selkies, though many even here don't believe the stories," said the human. "My grandmother was a selkie, as a matter of fact. She never went back to the sea after she fell in love with my grandfather."

That caught her attention. "No...sea?"

The girl nodded excitedly. "That's right! She stayed here on land, with us. But she told me stories of her life before and I have waited my whole life for a chance to meet one of my kin from the sea."

Blinking, Cascadia studied the young woman in front of her. Tan skin and wide, dark eyes, her hair the color of coral. A descendent of a selkie who had made her trip to land and never returned? One of those her elders said had been killed by humans, or made to choose between their children and the sea?

"What do they call you?" Emmy asked, bouncing in her seat as she took her hand.

"Aaahh-ah-aah," Cascadia attempted to sing the melody of her name the way she would beneath the sea, but it sounded strange and unfamiliar on her tongue.

"Hmm," said Emmy, tilting her head to the side to study her. "Would it be alright if we just call you Marina for now?"

She nodded. The towering human appeared beside her again, another small bucket in his hand. This one had no top, and Cascadia could see a dark brown liquid within. Carefully, she picked up the bottle and took the smallest of sips. Warm, smooth deliciousness coursed over her tongue and she looked down in surprise. The flavor she had no words for and the sweetness that brightened on her lips was an entirely new sensation.

With a smile, Cascadia sipped slowly on the warm liquid. She observed the other humans who entered the small building, where they requested their own little buckets of warm liquids from the tall land dweller. David. As they sat, Emmy chattered.

"You must have so many questions! You should come stay with Grandma and I. I can pull out the trundle bed for you," the girl rambled.

"Stay? You?" Cascadia felt out the words carefully, hoping she understood correctly.

"Yes! You can sleep at my house. Grandma will be so happy to see another selkie," Emmy explained. "We'll keep your fur safe. I can show you around Seaside!"

"Sea...side," the selkie tested the sound.

"That's our town. Seaside, Oregon. Just at the edge of the sea, surrounded by water on three sides," continued the girl.

"El...elder. Gran-Mar. Like me?" Cascadia focused on making the human sounds, mimicking the girl's speech as closely as she could.

When Emmy nodded excitedly, relief flooded through her. The girl's bright, coral colored hair caught the light and sparkled like that thing the elders warned of—fire. If a ship caught fire, even way out in the open sea, the whole thing could be destroyed and every land dweller on board, too. She had wondered why humans would keep using such a dangerous thing.

But in this place, as the young woman told her about the machine that made their hot liquids and warmed foods, she reluctantly admitted it might have its benefits. During a lull in orders, when his machines finally stopped making such a racket, David brought them brown things that looked like parchment.

"Chocolate croissants! Thanks, David." Emmy smiled widely at her. "Marina, you're going to love these. It's a baked good, sweet and fluffy."

She stared blankly at the pastry the girl held out to her. Those words were unfamiliar, so she had no idea what to expect. Nevertheless, Cascadia picked one up and sniffed it. It smelled of the same scent as her warm liquid, a flavor that did not exist under the sea.

When she bit into the treat, her eyes rolled back and she sighed happily.

"See? Good, right? It's buttery dough and chocolate pieces, all warm and melty from the oven," the girl continued between mouthfuls.

"Ch-chock-latt?" Cascadia sounded it out. "Chocklatt sweet."

"Exactly! Your drink there is hot chocolate, which is just a liquid version of chocolate." Emmy smiled brightly.

"Drink. Drink?" She held up her small bucket.

"Yes! Your drink is hot chocolate, and you drink it from your cup. If you get too cold again, you just ask David for a hot chocolate," the other girl explained. "You're catching on quickly!"

After a while, when Cascadia felt well and truly warm again after her night out in the snow, Emmy asked if she was ready to go home. Startled, she had shook her head vehemently, insisting she could not return to the sea yet. A giggle from the girl surprised her.

"No, no. Not to your home. Will you come to my home, Marina?" Emmy asked softly.

"Your...home," said Cascadia, feeling out the sounds. "Gran-Mah? Like me?"

"That's right! Come home with me and meet my grandmother. She can help you adjust while you're here on land." Emmy nodded.

And so the pair had bid farewell to the tall, dark-haired land dweller called David. Cascadia's dark brown eyes took in every detail as she followed the young woman back out into the cold, white world beyond the little room. The place was bustling now, humans of all shapes and sizes hurrying past them, like fish caught in a tide.

The many layers of cloth that Emmy had wrapped her in earlier did a surprisingly good job of keeping Cascadia warm on their walk, despite the chill of the wind.They passed the end of the Boardwalk and stepped out onto the snow-covered ground.

Emmy led her past several other structures she could not name or make sense of, keeping up a consistent dialogue even if Cascadia only grasped maybe half of what she said. At the edge of the forest, a small pointed shape came into view. There, just tucked into the treeline, stood a little building that Emmy tugged her toward.

"It isn't much, but it's home. Our little A-frame cabin. It has everything we need."

Snow covered the two sloping sides of the roof. A wooden door with a wreath of green was suddenly all that stood between Cascadia and an elder who had chosen to spend her life on land. One who had forsaken their kind to remain here, in this place, with her children born of a human father.

It felt as if she were only a moment away from being swept into a current too strong for her to escape. As if, once she stepped into this place and spoke to this person, Cascadia's life would take a turn. It might never be the same again.

The warm air of the cottage hit Cascadia like a wall as she stepped into the small space, following Emmy. When the young woman immediately removed several layers of her winter gear, the selkie followed suit. She mimicked the girl's steps, placing the biggest layer on the little hook by the door and the smaller pieces into the little pouch.

"Gran! I'm home," Emmy called cheerfully. "And we have a visitor."

A stooped old woman with white hair pulled back at the nape of her neck stood at the window, staring out at the churning waves with her hands tucked behind her back. She seemed to wake from a daze, turning to greet the girl. But when her eyes snagged on Cascadia, the woman froze, her smile falling away.

"This is Marina! David and I found her earlier, wandering all by herself in the cold," rambled Emmy as she tugged the selkie toward the older land dweller.

For the longest heartbeat of her life, Cascadia stared into the liquid brown eyes of one of her kind. An elder who had been lost to the humans so many moons ago. While her face and form were unrecognizable to the selkie, those dark, soulful eyes were unmistakeable. All she could do was blink at the sight of her mother's best friend.

The wail that emerged from the woman's lips as she lifted both hands to cover her mouth was a feral, desperate thing. When she collapsed to her knees, Emmy rushed to her side, overcome with worry. But her eyes never left Cascadia's, not even for a moment.

"H-how?" gasped the old woman. "It cannot be. After all these years."

"You...no sea...moons ago," Cascadia forced out the human words she had begun to grasp over the course of her first day on land. "You...here? Daughter?"

"Yes, I have been on land this entire time, raising my children." The old woman nodded.

"Only...daughters..." managed Cascadia, turning to look at Emmy.

At that, the woman chuckled. "We can only have daughters, that's right. I had one precious daughter with the man I fell in love with, before he died. Cancer, it was. A land disease."

"No...sea?" Cascadia stared her down, voice becoming steadier. "No human. Find fur. Home."

"I could not leave her. She was only five years old, and born on land." The old woman reached for her granddaughter's hand, squeezing tight.

"Gran took care of Mama all on her own, in this house that Grandpa built for them," Emmy spoke up, voice quivering. "When Mama fell in love at sixteen and got pregnant with me, she had dreams of a family thriving under this roof."

"Where mother?" demanded Cascadia, looking back and forth between the pair.

"She...died. Giving birth to me." Tears filled Emmy's eyes as she looked away.

"Her father had no interest in providing for a child without a wife to do the work," the older woman explained carefully. "On land, only women raise children. Men work long days at sea or travel far for work. So he left Emmy here with me, and never looked back."

A burning rage filled Cascadia at those words. She could not comprehend leaving behind a child. Every tale of warning told to the selkies was about a mother whose love for her children surpassed even her love for the sea. In all of Cascadia's moons, the possibility of abandoning a child had not crossed her mind.

Could human men truly be such callous, selfish creatures? No wonder this selkie had remained on land long after she had reclaimed her fur. The thought of what she must have endured, trapped in this form, unable to return home. Her heart broke, knowing she had been only steps away from the sea and her kin.

"Here, child, I have something for you," the old woman said.

Cascadia watched as she pulled a few vials down from a shelf and set a kettle to boil. Again, she marveled at the land dwellers' everyday use of the fire she knew to be wild and dangerous. This selkie had been on land long enough to become accustomed to it.

Would she do the same before she returned to the sea? A sharp whistle interrupted her thoughts, causing Cascadia to look around the room in confusion.

"It's just the teapot. That means it's ready," Emmy explained, patting her hand.

The old woman dropped leaves and other bits that she did not recognize into little dishes. Billowing smoke followed the steaming water, a sight she did not understand. A sweet floral scent wafted through the air and Cascadia inhaled deeply.

She reached for the handle on the small dish the woman had set before her, but Emmy forced her hand back down. Blinking at the girl, Cascadia waited for another explanation.

"It's too hot right now. Like the coffee earlier, from David," the girl said quickly.

"You need to let it steep a while," added Emmy's grandmother. "When it is ready, it will help you communicate more smoothly. I bestowed a bit of my knowledge from my years on land into those flowers, back when I still had traces of magic."

Emmy's eyes lit up, her smile wide. "You had magic, Gran?"

"A long time ago..." spoke the old woman softly.

"Magic. Fur. Selkie. Home," Cascadia said, understanding dawning on her.

"Yes, child. When I realized I could not go home, I imbued the magic that would have transformed me to my true form into this brew," she explained. "Marsh marigold, Water Forget-Me-Nots, Lotus, Coast Lily, and Water Lily. Plants that thrive near the sea."

The bouquet smelled like home, she realized. Like all the beautiful things that bloomed at the water's edge and the plants that thrived in the open ocean. What a clever thing to have done. Cascadia smiled at the old woman, reaching out to touch her weathered and wrinkled hand.

And then the circle was complete. Emmy held both of their hands, sitting between them as the link between their worlds. A tingle worked its way from her fingertips through her body. Her toes twitched at the unfamiliar feeling—she had experienced it only once, the day she had transformed. But this time it came without pain or shock, only a warm tingling sensation.

"Now you may drink," the old woman said.

And so each of them picked up their little dishes with the delicate handles and took a long, slow sip of the steeped tea. Words, images, sounds, danced in Cascadia's mind as she sat there. Memories from the selkie who had been lost to the sea flooded her mind as though she had been beside her in the very moment.

All of it seemed to hit her at once, a breaking wave straight to her strange new lungs. Cascadia slumped in her chair, struggling to keep her eyes open. But the old woman shook her head, instructing Emmy to help her to the couch.

"Rest now, child," she whispered. "In the morning, it will make more sense."

At that, Cascadia allowed herself to drift away on the sea of memories and feelings. Her heart slowed and her head lolled as she lost consciousness. Only darkness remained.

Tricky Little Beasts

NORTH

The early morning sunlight slanted in through the blinds and slowly pulled North from his restful night of sleep. He blinked open his crystal blue eyes, taking in the room around him sleepily. At first, he thought he must still be dreaming.

Then the realization hit him like a snowball to the head: he wasn't home in the North Pole. He had made it to a human town, wherever Mrs. Claus had sent him via Comet and a mini sleigh. The luxurious sheets and quilted comforter had made it the best sleep he'd had in ages.

Running one hand through his shoulder-length blonde hair, North Snowstorm grinned from ear to pointy ear. This elf had finally made his dream come true, with a little help and Christmas magic. He would get to see the human world up close and personal for the next 30 days.

After that, North could return home, curiosity satiated and adventure had. His cookie-cutter life, planned out long before his birth, would be bearable with the memory of his adventures to hold onto. As a Snowstorm, he would continue the tradition of gift wrapping presents for Christmas, beside his father and older brother.

But for these few precious weeks, the world was his oyster. Scrambling out of bed, North tugged on a pair of pants followed by a warm sweater. He peeked into the bathroom mirror to make sure his hair wasn't too mussed for company, smiled at his snowflake patterned sweater. He whistled along to "Let It Snow" as he skipped down the stairs.

In the lobby, he found Ms. Eve sitting behind the front desk, her pointed ears on full display as a result of her chignon. North smiled at the sight.

"Good morning, Mr. Snowstorm."

"Good morning to you, Ms. Eve!" He replied cheerily. "Tell me everything I need to see and do around town."

The sweet older woman plucked a few brochures off her desk and handed them to him. "We have plenty to do on the Boardwalk, a national park, and an aquarium. Could I get you a coffee to start your day?"

"Oh, yes, please," North nodded vigorously.

That was when he noticed the little coffee maker in the back corner of her workspace. A two tiered tray held pumps with various flavors of syrups to add to his coffee. This had been one of the things he had dreamt of trying—all the customized drinks not available back home.

North watched with wide blue eyes as Ms. Eve bustled about, setting the machine and pouring in the ground coffee beans.

"What'll it be this morning, then?" She gestured to the

display. "I could whip you up a peppermint mocha, or a gingerbread latte, or even a hot chocolate, if you prefer."

"Gingerbread latte? Yes, please," exclaimed North.

When the proprietor pulled a number of small jars from under the counter, all he could do was watch in fascination. Ms. Eve measured out some brown sugar, tossed it in a Christmas tree mug, and added a pinch of cinnamon, ginger, and cloves. She stirred them gently before adding a little dollop of molasses and a splash of vanilla extract.

Her little coffee machine dinged and she reached for the steamed milk, giving everything a good turn to mix properly. Then she swiped the little cup from her machine and poured the shots of espresso right into the mug with the rest. Before he had even processed it, Ms. Eve had topped it with a single gingerbread man and a little spoon.

"There you are, young man." The woman winked, her cherry cheeks bright with mirth.

North stared down into the Christmas tree mug in absolute amazement. The warmth of the latte spread to his palms and he soaked up every bit of it. With one hand, he carefully dipped his gingerbread man into the piping hot cup of coffee. As soon as the cookie hit his tongue, it crumbled into soft, moist pieces and the spices danced on his tastebuds.

He took a careful sip of the steaming mug and sighed happily.

"It tastes exactly like a gingerbread cookie!"

"I'll be sure to send the recipe home with you." Ms. Eve patted his hand. "You should bring something new and magical to that old place when you go home."

The thrill of adventure coursed through North's veins as

he sipped the delicious hot beverage and planned out his day. He wanted to see everything the town had to offer, and maybe even go further out if the chance arose. For the moment, he settled for a trip to the lighthouse on the edge of the sea.

Daily tours about the history of the place and how the town had sprung up around it were offered, with one starting in about an hour. Savoring the last few drops of his gingerbread latte, North turned to Ms. Eve.

"That was absolutely magical! Thanks ever so much."

He set his mug on the counter, donned his coat, and pulled a knitted hat over his ears. Sufficiently warded against the cold, North waved goodbye to his hostess and headed out into the bright, snowy day. The sun glittered off the snowflakes and frost, blinding in its magnificence.

The walk from the North Pole Bed & Breakfast to the lighthouse took only forty minutes at a brisk pace. With a determined step and snow-proof boots, he headed toward the beach. The wisps of his blonde hair that peeked out from under his hat blew around with the crisp wind off the ocean, sometimes blocking his view.

Undeterred, North Snowstorm marched on. He spotted the lighthouse as soon as he crested the first big hill. A tall, weathered white building with a rusted metal case holding a large bulb sat on the top of a massive cliffside overlook. Just ahead, he could make out the parking lot and entrance to Ecola State Park.

Trees taller than he had ever seen reached toward the sky as he stepped into the park. North tipped his head all the way back to stare straight up at the canopy so far above his head. Even in the dead of winter, the view could only be described as breathtaking.

Families drove by in their minivans and campers heading further in, to the main visitor's center. But North kept his icy blue eyes trained on that lighthouse in the distance. He meandered through the dense forest alone, enjoying the sounds of the animals in the underbrush and the birds high above.

A pair of deer crossed his path, pausing to determine if he posed a threat to them. When North made no effort to move closer, they seemed to determine he could be trusted. He watched as they ambled through the winter forest, long legs agile and eyes sharp.

Finally, he came to an overlook with a wooden bench and a spectacular view of the Pacific Ocean. The lighthouse, now defunct and nearly impossible for humans to reach, sat straight ahead on its little island made of rocks. A number of wooden signs were posted along one side of the overlook, telling the story of Terrible Tilly, the Tillamook Rock Lighthouse.

The brisk seaside breeze ruffled his hair as North settled onto the bench. In the distance, a squirming pile of seals were beached upon the rocks surrounding the lighthouse. The water below crashed in waves against the steep cliffs, turning from deepest blue to pale seafoam. He could have sat there for hours, watching the birds dive for fish and listening to the seals holler.

His blue eyes shuttered closed as he inhaled the smell of the salty sea. If North could capture this moment in time, keep it forever, he would. These were the moments he wished he had his mother's artistic talents—even the ability to crochet this scene to hold it close to his heart would be better than letting the memory fade.

Eventually, face chapped by the wind, North decided he needed to get out of the winter air. His sturdy snowboots helped him pick his way back through the snow-covered forest without stumbling, his thick winter coat zipped to his chin to keep out the cold. Though he passed a few people, it seemed many humans did not venture out in weather like this.

North tugged his knitted cap further down, covering his forehead and ears more securely. As a Christmas elf, he knew a thing or two about cold. He had grown up in the North Pole, after all. But most of his cozy life in his little village was spent indoors, with roaring fires and warm cider. He could not fault the humans for seeking warmth and shelter as the animals did.

"They say the dark waters of this place hold secrets the likes of which you can't imagine," a gruff voice called out. "Maidens born of seafoam, more creature than woman. Generations of them live here, mingled with our own children."

On the beach, a wrinkled old sailor shouted to a crowd of onlookers. His voice, as weathered as his face, sounded like sandpaper being rubbed against wood. North slowed his pace, curious about the strange story the man told. He stepped to the edge of the crowd, made up of maybe a dozen or so humans of varying ages.

Though North leaned left and then right, and stretched up onto his tiptoes, he struggled to get a good view of the sailor from his position at the back of the group. Back home, North was considered rather tall; he had forgotten that the average human these days stood several inches taller than him. As he fidgeted in an attempt to get a better look, the old man continued.

"I know you lot want to believe in beautiful women with fish tails and faces like angels, but that's not what you'll find here in Seaside. No heavenly voices to lure you into the sea where they might drown you and steal your soul," rambled the sailor.

"If they're not mermaids, what are they?" Someone asked.

"Selkies, lad," barked the man. "Seals with magic that turns them human, gives them legs and the body of a woman so convincing you'd never know she was a feral thing until it's too late."

"That doesn't sound so bad," a teenager whispered to his friend, grinning.

"Legend has it that they come to land in search of a husband, because they cannot procreate without our help. But if they do not return to the sea before their pregnancy comes to term, the child born will be unable to transform," the sailor continued.

"Well, if they need men to make babies, does that mean none of them like girls?" a young woman asked.

The old man sputtered at that, flustered. "They are here for a purpose! They are not seeking love or affection—they need us to keep their species alive. Does that not concern you?"

"Why should it?" North felt compelled to speak up suddenly. "Should you prefer to doom their kind to extinction simply because they are different from you?"

Every face in the crowd swiveled toward him. Straightening his spine and holding his chin high, the elf addressed the group as a whole. Not a whisper worked through the assembly as they waited with bated breath for his next words.

"If they need your help for survival, is that such a bad thing? Do you not have enough land and resources to share?"

"It ain't about that!" the old sailor shouted. "They're dangerous. They use us and disappear with our children, unless you know the secret to keeping them. Tricky little beasts!"

"What's the secret?" several voices called out.

"You must find their fur, their seal pelt, and hide it where they can never find it. Then they will be trapped in their human form and their children will be born on land, perfectly healthy," grumbled the sailor.

North could only shake his head at the strange superstition. In a world with magic like Santa Claus and elves, it hardly seemed far-fetched to believe that such creatures existed. Especially in a place like this, surrounded by the sea and boasting thousands of seals on their beaches.

The idea of holding someone against their will, taking away such a major part of their identity, did not sit well with North. He might not have the same passion for wrapping perfect gifts that his father did, but the idea of never being allowed to gift wrap another present for the rest of his life felt like a death sentence.

For all that he had longed to see the world beyond the edges of the North Pole, North had not once considered the possibility of being unable to return home. Of someone else keeping him here, far from his family, for the rest of his days. His heart ached at the thought.

If there were beautiful sea creatures walking among the humans in this town beside the sea, they deserved their freedom and heritage as much as he did. His steps carried him away from the group and the loud sailor with his ominous warnings.

Up ahead, he could make out the wooden pier with its little shops and carousel. The glowing Boardwalk sign, the music from the children's ride, the happy chatter of people meandering about drew him in like a ship to shore. North took in the sights and sounds of the gaily decorated place, all garlands and Christmas lights and falling snow.

He spotted a coffee shop on his right and headed in that direction. A warm drink and a chance to get out of the cold would cheer him right up.

As North stepped into Holly Jolly Coffee, he breathed in the wonderful scent of freshly ground coffee and baked goods warming in the toaster oven. The little cafe had white walls and wooden accents, with a Christmas tree in the far corner covered in seashells and mermaid ornaments. He stepped closer to inspect the sparkling pieces.

One ornament in particular caught his eye. It was a mermaid with dark hair and darker eyes, and a tail the shade of melted chocolate. Not a colorful, magical mermaid, then. He wondered if this was one of the selkies of legend in this region. A voice over his shoulder startled him into nearly dropping the pretty trinket.

"She's beautiful, isn't she?"

A tall, dark-haired young man stood behind North, watching him. His smile was easy and his eyes seemed to sparkle with mirth; the elf got the feeling he could trust this human. Straightening, he held out one hand and smiled when the other man shook it.

"I'm visiting from out of town," explained North. "Can you tell me more about this ornament?"

"Absolutely! That there is a seal-woman, known around these parts as a selkie," the young man replied.

"Are they...real?"

"You know, I would have said no if you'd asked me yesterday." The man rubbed the back of his head and chuckled. "But, as a matter of fact, I met one myself just this morning."

North raised one bushy blonde eyebrow. "You're not just pulling my leg?"

"I'm David. I've lived here all my life and grew up on these stories, and I always thought it was a fanciful tale, to be honest," continued the young man, placing the ornament back on the tree.

"Until today?" asked North breathlessly.

"I knew the minute I saw her, I swear it to ya." David lowered his voice. "Eyes like molten chocolate, dark and deep as the sea. Hair like mocha waves, tumbling down her back and shoulders nearly to her waist. A sharp animal-like awareness in her movements."

For a moment, North struggled to reply. "That was so... eloquent. You really thought all that when you saw her?"

"I did. I called my cousin Emmy straightaway to come and get her, since Emmy insists her Gran was a selkie many years ago," explained David. "Thought she was making it up, til I saw that girl wander in here this morning."

"That's quite the story, friend," the elf followed him back to the front counter.

"It's been an exciting day. What can I get'cha?"

"Do you have any Christmas drinks?" North leaned his head back, craning his neck to look up at the menu.

"We do! You want something classic like a peppermint mocha? Or something new, like the salted pretzel cocoa latte?" asked David with a smile.

"New! Definitely something new. That sounds lovely."

North reached into his pocket to pull out the paper money and metal coins that Mrs. Claus had provided him for his time among humans. He would need to pay with these instead of the for-the-good-of-all system the elves used back home. His first time using the new currency.

David took the bills, punched some buttons on his register, and handed back what North assumed must be his change. He stuffed the bills back into his pocket and walked over to the seating area in front of the Christmas tree.

The hustle and bustle of people passed him by like background noise as North shrugged off his coat and settled into the leather seat. Automatically, he pulled off his hat and tucked it into his jacket pocket. Knowing that his hair surely looked like a bird's nest, he ran both hands through the blonde locks to work out the knots.

"Here you are," David said brightly as he set the hot latte on the table in front of North.

He did a double-take as he stepped away, turning back quickly. North tilted his head back to look up at the much taller young man from his spot on the comfy chair.

"W-where did you say you're visiting from, fella?"

"Oh, way up north. Little bitty town," North informed him politely. "Barely a dot on a map."

"Uh-huh. Right," David mumbled.

He stretched out for a while on the comfortable chair,

just observing the everyday human lives unfolding around him. People-watching. The term made a lot more sense to him now. North saw a mother with a double stroller, toddlers all bundled up, grabbing a large hot peppermint mocha with two shots of espresso.

The children fussed in their seats, desperately trying to escape. As the mother asked David to add two pastries to her order, North found himself drawn like a magnet to the kids.

"Hi there! What's your name?" he asked cheerfully.

The two small humans responded with gibberish that North couldn't make sense of. Their mother laughed, translating for him.

"Riley and Rachel. They're two."

"Have you been good this year, Rachel and Riley?" North asked.

Both little cherub faces nodded vigorously, their brown hair bouncing with the movement. He smiled down at them, producing two miniature candy canes from his pocket. Wide blue eyes stared longing at the treats as North turned to their mother.

"Is it alright if I give them a treat?"

The woman hesitated for a moment, then replied, "Okay, you seem nice enough."

"Straight from the North Pole!" North whispered to the tots as he handed them over.

"Are you a Christmas elf?" The mother studied him more carefully. "I wasn't aware we had a Santa at the Boardwalk."

He rubbed the back of his neck with one palm, chuckling. "Something like that. Scoping the place out for the Big Man in Red."

That seemed to satisfy the woman, who then opened

each tiny candy and handed them back to her waiting toddlers. David called out a name and she turned, raising one hand.

"Your large hot peppermint mocha, ma'am," the young man said. "Come back soon!"

With that, the woman bustled her toddlers, stroller, hot coffee back out onto the main Boardwalk. North raised one hand in a slight wave as they turned away. One of the children stared back, not taking their eyes off the elf. For fun, North tugged his hat off and showed the tot his ears. Big blue eyes and a shocked expression were his reward.

Behind the counter, he could feel David's keen eyes on him, too. He quickly tucked his hat back over his pointed ears and hurried back to his cozy little spot and his coffee.

They Called Me Nerissa

CASCADIA

Sunlight filtered in through the window of the A-frame house, where Cascadia had slept away most of the evening and night on Emmy's couch. The little cottage was just big enough for the two of them and if she had had any possessions there would not have been room. As she sat up, slowly, she realized she could hear the roar of the crashing waves.

When she turned toward the window the old woman stared out of the night before, she saw the sea in all its frigid, powerful glory. The sea met the sky, the rising sun reflected in sparkling droplets and shades of orange. Cascadia smiled at the sight of her home.

"Good morning, Marina!" Emmy chirped, rushing into the room.

"G-Good...morning," the selkie parroted back the words, surprised.

Then the girl's grandmother walked into the living room and looked at her with those deep, dark, soulful eyes. A vision of last night's joined hands and steeped tea came back to her. Cascadia blinked several times, trying to recall the details.

"We should see how much the tea has done to help you adjust," the old woman said.

"Oh, that's right!" cried Emmy.

Not quite understanding, Cascadia followed the woman across the room and into the kitchen. When she pointed at an object, the selkie answered with words unfamiliar to her.

"Kettle."

A nod. A small smile. Another pointed finger.

"Table."

On and on they went, the old woman testing the extent of which her magic had transmuted her years of life on land into words the selkie could understand and replicate. Emmy watched them, fascination written plainly on her face.

"What is your name, child?"

She hesitated for only a moment before the word came to her. "Cascadia. Eldest daughter of Neve."

"Oh, that's so pretty!" Emmy squealed.

"I knew it the moment I saw you. Neve's daughter," said the old woman sadly. "You were but a wee thing when I took my voyage to the dry land."

"My mother remains heartbroken at the loss of you," Cascadia replied earnestly.

"They called me Nerissa in those days. I go by Marissa now," the woman explained.

Behind her, Emmy perked up. "Is that why my full name is Emmalynne? Is it a selkie name?"

Her grandmother turned a sad smile toward the girl. Cascadia wondered at the two of them, so close and full of love. A little pod all their own. A family. All this time, while her own mother thought Nerissa had been trapped on land by a cruel fisherman, she had in fact been tending to her daughter and granddaughter.

Though the words were still strange to her, Cascadia found that the human phrases came to her from somewhere she couldn't explain. The words she would have used below the sea, to speak to her own pod, seemed to translate directly in her mind without any trouble. The last of the elder's magic, indeed.

"You gave me your words," the selkie said, turning to her.

"I knew I could not go home," the woman called Marissa frowned. "I took a chance to funnel that magic into the tea. In case such a day ever came."

"And here I am." Cascadia smiled softly at her.

"So you are, child. As if the moon foretold it to me in a dream." Marissa patted her hand gently.

Then the elder instructed her to follow her around the kitchen, teaching her the basics of the oven and stove. Showing her how to heat the milk in the little saucepan. Cascadia scooped the brown powder into the simmering milk as told, then Marissa added a few other things.

Without prompting, Emmy hurried to the cupboard and pulled out three matching white mugs. The girl lined them up on the counter beside her gran and stepped back, out of the way. When Marissa poured the steaming milky drink into their cups, she simply stared.

Before Cascadia had a chance to say anything, Emmy had pulled another container down from the cupboard. She sprinkled a little powder over the liquid, just as she had done yesterday.

"Cinnamon! You should always add a pinch of cinnamon to your hot cocoa," giggled Emmy.

"It is good for this human form, in many ways." Marissa set each cup on the table.

After allowing a few minutes for the boiling liquid to cool, Cascadia watched the others pick up their mugs and take a sip. She followed suit. Just like the day before, the deliciously sweet and creamy treat warmed her body as it danced brightly on her tongue.

"Your fire makes this possible?" she asked the old woman.

"It certainly has its benefits," laughed Marissa. "As well as the heater keeping the room warm so we don't freeze our toes off!"

It was only then that the selkie realized why the insides of buildings were far more comfortable than the spaces outside. Hidden from her sight, small fires controlled the warmth. Cascadia had never considered such a thing before.

The selkies simply adjusted to the temperature of the water at the differing times of year. They grew plumper as winter approached, putting on blubber to ward against the cold. It happened naturally, her body simply knowing what to do.

But the humans had no such feature in their strange furless bodies. It seemed they had come up with a way to fix that, in certain circumstances. Surprisingly clever of them.

"Want to explore?" Emmy asked brightly, grinning.

Cascadia nodded quickly. She wanted to see more of the human world, more of this land above the waves. The two bundled up again in all their winter layers and bid goodbye to Marissa.

"Have fun storming the castle!" the old woman called as she waved.

"What?" asked the selkie, utterly lost.

"Oh, it's just a line from our favorite movie," Emmy explained.

The vague concept of a movie came to her mind, courtesy of the magic Marissa had shared. Storytelling was the preferred method of entertainment among the selkies, with dramatic reenactments occasionally adding to the fun. Cascadia wondered if she would get a chance to watch a movie during her time on land.

The young woman with the coral-colored hair led her toward the beach. Cascadia admired the view of the sea from this new vantage point, the way it seemed to go on forever, from the beach in front of them way out to the horizon. It felt like that when she was in the water, too. She liked that the feeling remained the same.

Emmy pointed to a paper on a pole just ahead of them.

"It's beach clean up day!"

"What is that?" Cascadia tilted her head in confusion.

"There's this wonderful local ocean conservation group that comes out once a month to collect any trash out on the beach," the girl continued. "They do lots of stuff to try to protect the planet and the ocean. But this is the only one I get to help with."

The selkie considered this for a long moment. "You have humans who...take care of the sea? Make it better?"

"Yup!" Emmy replied enthusiastically.

With that, she picked up her pace, hurrying toward the section of the waterfront that faced a small parking lot. Cascadia did her best to keep up, her legs still strange and new to her. But the knowledge instilled in her through Marissa's magic helped her understand how her human form worked. It kept her going with far more ease than the day before.

Up ahead, a handful of land dwellers had gathered at the edge of the beach. It seemed they had all arrived in the same car and they were waiting for something.

"Emmy!" someone called out.

A girl with warm, dark skin and ebony hair waved at them. Her coat and boots were a soft, pretty pink that complimented her skin tone beautifully. The sight made Cascadia wonder where such items came from. Would she need to get her own clothing? Surely she could not borrow Emmy's things forever.

The girls hugged when they reached her and Emmy gestured to Cascadia.

"Aria, this is my cousin, Cascadia."

"Nice to meet you. What a pretty name," replied Aria with a smile.

Unsure how best to respond, Cascadia nodded and returned her smile. She simply observed as the two girls chatted after that, her dark eyes constantly drawn back out to sea as if it were calling her home. The pull felt like a physical thing, a thread tugging at her heart.

"I'm so glad you made it out today," Emmy told Aria.

"Me, too! It's always more fun with good company."

A few more vehicles pulled into the parking lot, stopping near where they stood. People tumbled out, men and women of all ages, as Cascadia took in the diverse group. The waves crashed loudly to her left, distracting her from the conversations around her. Emmy introduced her to more people, explaining that she was a cousin visiting from far away. That seemed to be enough for those present, who asked no other questions.

Several people pulled out long banners and strung them up between the cars. She studied them until the words took shape in her mind: save our oceans. Cascadia felt the hope buoy in her chest at that. A group of land dwellers who wanted to protect the seas.

She wondered how she ought to bring up the topic, turning to Emmy with her questions.

"How can I help save the oceans?"

"Well, this is always a big help," the girl replied. "Do you mean on a larger scale?"

"More. Bigger. Yes." Cascadia searched for the words to express her thoughts.

"Well, the woman in charge is over there in the black jacket," Emmy added.

"Help me," the selkie declared.

She took off at a steady march toward the person identified, forcing Emmy to jog for a moment to catch up to her.

"Excuse me," Cascadia announced when they reached her. "I want to help save the sea."

"That's great! What did you have in mind?" replied the woman with a warm smile.

"I know where the fish should be. I know when something bad is in the water. I can help," insisted the selkie passionately.

When the organizer turned to Emmy, she seemed to ask silent questions. The girl informed her that Cascadia was her cousin, raised mostly way up north, away from civilization. Nodding, the woman raised one eyebrow gracefully.

"You know a lot about the migration patterns and sea life in this area?"

"Yes," cried Cascadia. "I know everything."

At that, the woman chuckled. "Everything, huh? Well, then. I'm Suzanne and I am the Marine Conservation Manager for Oregon Shores. It sounds like we should discuss employment opportunities available at the company."

"Thank you so much! That would be great," Emmy quickly interjected, shushing Cascadia.

"Here's my card. Get in touch by email. I would love to follow up," Suzanne said.

Then she turned back to her crew and began instructing volunteers on their assignments. Emmy pulled the selkie away from the group, eyes wide.

"She just offered you a job!"

"What is a job?" Cascadia asked.

"It means she wants to find a place for you to work with them, helping save the oceans," explained Emmy excitedly. "I'll show you their website and look at the job listings tonight."

Still not entirely sure what all of those words meant, Cascadia nodded. Her dark hair billowed out from under her jacket hood and she gazed longingly at the tide as it ebbed. If she could help the land dwellers who took care of the ocean, if she could change things up here on land, her pod of selkies would have much better odds of survival.

It seemed Cascadia had successfully taken the first step toward that goal.

She's Visiting

NORTH

For the rest of the day, North Snowstorm wandered around the Boardwalk, taking in the sights and sounds of the people around him. In the distance, he could just make out the lighthouse down the coast. On these weathered planks, though, the sound of crashing waves and noisy gulls drew his attention to the beach below.

Out in the water, somewhere just beyond the surface, there were seals who could turn into women. Magical creatures, like him. Hidden from humans for all these years. North couldn't get the image out of his head—a dark-haired woman with deep brown eyes, beautiful and wild. Stories of such creatures had not reached his village way up north.

He smiled to himself, leaning against the pier and staring out at the endless blue of the sea. In North's wildest dreams of seeing the modern human world, he had never considered the possibility of finding other magical creatures hiding in plain sight.

Ms. Eve had lived here among the humans for years,

running her little bed and breakfast with its year-round Christmas theme. It made North wonder if she, too, had been overcome with a need to see the world beyond the limits of their village in the North Pole. Could such a future be built?

Had Ms. Eve lived alone in this dreary, salt-swept place for all these years? North could not recall any whispers about an elf who had left the village in all his years. Something like that surely would have caught his attention. Which begged the question: how long had the elf lived here, away from their kind?

What had seemed like an impossibility just days ago suddenly felt tangible to North. His hands curled and uncurled around the wooden pier, his bright eyes turned toward the waves as he let the sudden seed of hope bloom in his chest.

The world truly was so much bigger than he had realized, from his isolated little corner of the North Pole. Though he still missed his parents and brother, North found himself considering a life somewhere like this. Plenty of snow and cold in the winters, enough to feel like home.

He wondered if his family would consider coming to stay at the North Pole Bed & Breakfast someday. How he longed to show him all there was to see of the world beyond their village. They had never understood North's fascination with the human world, the wide array of opportunities and possibilities available.

The sound of shouting reached his ears, muffled only slightly by his knitted cap. North turned his ice blue eyes toward the sea, searching for the source of the noise. A cluster of people were gathering a ways down the beach.

They held signs on wooden sticks and banners that they worked to string up between lightposts on the trail near the water's edge. He strained to read them from this distance, curiosity absolutely piqued.

"Save our oceans!"

Many voices chanted in unison, over and over. Their signs went up and large bins were hauled out of vehicles, then dragged toward the sea. As North watched, the several dozen people split into smaller groups and began walking along the beach. Each person carried a woven bag and a strange tool. When he recognized it from toy production, North laughed.

They were metal and plastic sticks with handles, used to pick things up without bending over to retrieve them. While he had only seen them in the form of shark or dinosaur headed toy versions on Christmas wishlists of countless children. These far less colorful versions were effective; the crew fanned out and covered a ton of ground.

"Excuse me, what are they doing?" he asked a passing stranger in a yellow reflective vest.

"Them? Oh, that's Oregon Shores. Once a month, they comb the beach and remove any trash they can find. Good folks," the gruff-voiced man replied.

"Thank you," murmured North as the man hurried off.

At that, he decided he ought to go down and help them. What a good use of his days in town, before he returned home to his family. Cleaning up the oceans and making the world better. North smiled to himself as he hurried down the beach to the nearest person.

"Hey there!"

He waved his arm comically, drawing the attention of a woman in a black winter coat.

"Can I help you?" she asked, pausing her work.

"I would like to help. Is there something I can do?" North shouted.

"That would be lovely, fella," the woman replied. "Whenever one of those bins gets full, could you put it into that white truck over there?"

She gestured to a pickup truck, the back open and ready to haul stuff. Though North wasn't entirely sure he could lift one of those large black bins that high by himself, he nodded. With that, the woman went back to the task at hand.

North jogged the short distance to the bins at the center of their workstation and took stock of how full each bin was at the moment. Then he looked up and down the beach, where he spotted two older men heading back in his direction, full bags hoisted over their shoulders. They dumped their hauls into the nearest bin without hesitation.

"There ya go, sonny boy," said the older man with thin, greying hair.

"Need a hand with that?" asked the younger guy.

He looked strong and healthy, and several inches taller than North. The elf accepted his help, lifting one end of the full bin as he followed the other man toward the truck. Together, they got it up onto the truckbed and the stranger pushed it as far back as his long arms would go.

With a smile and a wave, he headed back to join his companion combing the beach. North walked back to his post, thrilled to have something physically engaging and fulfilling to do with his day. People bustled back and forth, dropping off more plastic waste. Someone always offered to help him carry the full bins when they saw it had reached its limits.

For the better part of an hour, nothing of notice happened. Just a friendly hello and the crinkle of plastic and a jaunty wave of goodbye. Soon, the last two bins would be filled to the brim, and he guessed the crew would call it quits.

North frowned when he realized his new adventure would be ending shortly. Just then, two girls who had been walking the farthest side of the beach to his left came up with their full bags of trash. The younger one had pretty red hair and a friendly smile. But the other girl made him stop in his tracks.

Her hair, a dark espresso brown, cascaded over her shoulders. Speckled with snow, it hung nearly to her knees. The hood of her white jacket had been thrown back and though her ears looked red with the cold, she seemed not to be bothered in the slightest.

As she approached, North found that he could not look away. Her friend said something that he missed as those dark, soulful eyes pulled him in. The noise of the beach faded away as she met his gaze, hers deep brown to his icy blue.

He surmised that she was quite short for a human. Shorter than him, even. The other Christmas elves might even consider her small in stature. But under that coat, North could make out the voluptuous curves of a woman. Her hips were wide, nearly even with her shoulders.

Tan skin with a warm glow brought out the depth of her expressive eyes. Freckles dotted her skin in a little arc over her nose. Suddenly, North could not remember how to speak.

"Well, I think that's it for us," said the red-headed girl with a nervous chuckle.

The elf shook himself, trying to clear his mind of the haze the other woman had inflicted upon him.

"That's great. Thank you."

But the dark-haired beauty did not turn to leave. Her eyes lingered on his face, her look of interest and curiosity not hard to read. Her companion looked back and forth between them several times, clearly unsure what to do in this scenario.

"I-I'm North," he announced too loudly. "It's lovely to meet you..."

"Emmy," said the girl with the red hair. "And this is my cousin, Cascadia. She's visiting."

"You don't say! I'm visiting for the first time as well." North stumbled over his words but gave them a winning smile.

"I visit from the sea," Cascadia said simply.

Emmy rushed to cover her mouth. "She, um, grew up along the coast north of here."

"Well, it's an honor to be here at the same time as you, Cascadia," North gave a little bow. "Could I take you out for coffee tomorrow, perchance?"

The beautiful woman made a sour face. "No coffee. Hot chocolate, please."

"How about tomorrow morning? She'll be at Holly Jolly Coffee on the Boardwalk at ten," Emmy answered for her.

"Magical! I mean, wonderful! I'll see you then." North beamed at them.

Even as they bid their goodbyes to the other volunteers and walked away from the beach, he noticed that Cascadia kept turning to look back at him. A small shy wave was all North got before the two girls disappeared from view.

Nonetheless, he did a little victory dance. Tomorrow, he had a date with a gorgeous woman. Who may or may not secretly be another magical creature like him.

Chocolate and Peppermint

CASCADIA

For the second morning in a row, Cascadia awoke on the couch in Emmy and her grandmother's cabin, covered in soft, fluffy blankets. The borrowed pajamas she had slept in her flannel, a pretty plaid pattern in navy and lighter blue. In fact, the blue was nearly the same shade as the handsome young man's eyes.

In her mind, a vision of the blonde-haired land dweller with his sparkling smile reappeared. Cascadia had never really interacted with men before, other than her brief interactions with David at the coffee shop the other day. But this had been something entirely different; she was drawn to him in a way she couldn't describe.

"Good morning, Cascadia!" Emmy called, turning on the coffee machine.

"Good morning," replied the selkie, more sure of herself this time.

"I'm going to make some coffee for gran and I. Would you like a hot chocolate?"

Nodding enthusiastically, Cascadia smiled at the girl. Her "cousin." She supposed that was as accurate a moniker as they could use, with her being the descendent of a selkie from her pod. The human understanding of cousins and blood relations still felt a bit hazy in her mind, but it seemed to explain just enough about their relationship.

Tentatively, she turned on the running water in the bathroom. Emmy had taken a shower the night before and explained about washing off the dirt and sweat. Her understanding from Marissa's shared memories implied that the process would be relaxing and good.

Once she had gotten the water to a comfortable temperature, she flipped the toggle as Emmy had shown her. Then Cascadia stepped out of her pajamas and dipped one foot carefully into the running water. Warm, soothing water washed over her. Taking a deep, fortifying breath, the selkie pulled aside the curtain and moved her entire body under the stream of running water.

"Mmm," Cascadia murmured aloud, pleasantly surprised.

She tried out the washing supplies the women kept in their shower, her vague understanding enough to go on for now. When she had finished washing every inch of her new human body for the first time, Cascadia leaned back against the wall. If she closed her eyes, she could pretend that she was out in the winter-cold sea with her sisters, racing through the waves.

Her heart squeezed tightly as she thought of them, back in their pod's underwater caves, probably worried sick about her. But Cascadia could not return to them yet—not without finding a way to make things better for the other selkies. As the eldest daughter in her family, it fell to her to protect the future of their pod.

"Cascadia, are you done?" Emmy called out, knocking on the bathroom door. "Your cocoa is ready and Gran is up."

A startled squeak escaped her as she reached for the faucet and swiftly shut off the flowing water. Wrapping a fluffy towel around herself like she had with her fur after she had first transformed, Cascadia stepped out of the shower and dried herself off. How strange to think that that had been just two sleeps ago and now, here she was, on land with lost kin.

Over breakfast, she decided to bring up the reason for her trip to land. Cascadia cleared her throat to ensure she had everyone's attention.

"Selkies are in danger," she said sadly. "Not enough fish. Too much garbage in the sea. Harder to come to land and make babies."

Marissa nodded, her expression serious. "I feared as much."

"Someone must do something. I must do something," Cascadia announced.

"What can you do?" asked Emmy, a tremble in her voice.

"You will help me work with the people who save the ocean, yes?" the selkie asked.

"Of course! We'll get you a job and you can help expand their efforts." Emmy's face lit up. "Is there anything else Gran and I can do to help you?

Cascadia tapped her fingers against her chin, thinking. "Need more selkies. Babies. Can you help with that?"

Across from her, Marissa coughed loudly. The old woman looked a bit shocked at the bluntness of the question.

"Selkies that get pregnant on land but return to the sea have selkie babies," Cascadia explained to Emmy. "If selkies stay on land, they have human babies."

"Are you saying you need someone to start a selkie dating service?" The girl giggled.

"Dating?" echoed the selkie, blinking in confusion.

"Today, you have a date with that handsome blonde man from last night," Emmy replied. "He will take you to eat and get to know each other. After a few dates, people usually... make babies."

Cascadia considered this. "Can you find human men who do not want to keep the selkies or the babies? Not trapped here, like Marissa."

"Oh. Well, I suppose that's easier now than it's ever been," said Emmy quietly.

"Good. I can tell my sisters to come to land, meet humans, and leave right away." The selkie nodded to herself, thinking out loud.

"I know you're upset about Emmy's father not wanting to keep her," Marissa began gently. "But if you want more selkie children, you must accept that these men do not want their babies."

She scowled at that, her freckles standing out against her burning red cheeks. "Humans no longer keep selkies forever. This is good."

"I suppose it's better than being stuck here when they want to return to the sea," said Emmy.

At that, all three women nodded in agreement. Cascadia

felt confident that she could use the magic gifted to her from Marissa and the support that she and Emmy provided to make the process easier for the rest of her pod. If the selkies knew that they had somewhere safe to stay, amongst their kin, and their furs would never be at risk of being stolen, perhaps they would be able to repopulate their kind after all.

Fixing the oceans would require far more work. She felt certain that someone needed to stay on land and assist the humans with the conservatory efforts. If she remained here with Emmy and Marissa, she could learn more about the human world and figure out how to restore the seas to their former glory.

While that idea had been preposterous only days ago, Cascadia realized now that staying on land with her cousin wouldn't be such a terrible thing after all. If she became the safe harbor for the other selkies, allowing them to thrive and repopulate, she suspected things would go far more smoothly than if each selkie simply wandered out of the sea alone and unsure.

Her thoughts seemed to form a path, a guide of what to do next to solve the selkies problems. But Emmy made a high-pitched screech and pointed to the clock.

"It's time to get ready! Your date with North is in an hour," the girl cried.

With Emmy's help, she put together an outfit that would keep her warm enough in this human form while still looking the human type of attractive to the young man. Black leggings hugged her curves and a dark blue sweater dress fell to her knees, wrapping all of her in soft, warm fabric. Her borrowed jacket and a matching pair of knee-high boots that just barely fit completed the look.

Then Cascadia found herself walking back across the snowy beach toward the Boardwalk. The midday hustle and bustle of countless land dwellers made her anxious, but she pushed herself to stand tall as Emmy had shown her. It seemed absurd that she had a date with an attractive human, in the midst of all the other more important things going on.

Meeting at the coffee shop, where David would be nearby and could call Emmy if needed, had been a good idea. Cascadia scanned the shop from the large window out front, looking for the blonde haired man she had met the night before. He stood near the front, leaning against the counter as he spoke to David.

She pushed through the door, fighting the strong gale coming off the sea. The two men stopped talking when she appeared, mouths open.

"Good morning," said Cascadia with a small smile.

"Good morning, indeed!" North replied, grinning. "I'm so glad you made it, Cascadia."

As they stood there watching each other, the tall human who ran the shop nodded at her. "Your usual, miss?"

Cascadia managed a nod and David disappeared behind his whirring machines, pushing buttons and making a racket. The promise of hot chocolate filled her with joy. She noticed that the blonde man, North, held a cup of his own. When he lifted it to take a drink, curiosity filled her.

"What do you drink?"

"Well, I love a good hot coffee on a day like this." North gave her a charming lopsided smile. "Today, it's a classic Peppermint Mocha. I love chocolate and peppermint together."

"P-Peppermint." Her voice wavered as she tried to recall the meaning.

Suddenly, he produced a small candy from his jacket pocket. It was red and white, a little stick with a curved end. Cascadia blinked in surprise, then reached for it. North carefully broke the plastic wrapper and handed the treat to her. She nibbled on the end of the candy cane.

The bright flavor shocked her. Cool, but dancing on her tongue like nothing she had ever eaten before. Remembering how much she had enjoyed the chocolate croissant the other day with Emmy, the selkie popped the whole candy into her mouth.

Her tongue tingled and she couldn't help the giggle she let out at the feeling.

"Yum!"

"It's good, isn't it?" North held up another small treat. "I can't believe you've never had a candy cane before."

Cascadia's dark eyes were full of mixed emotions as she glanced back at the handsome man across from her. "I come from far away. A very different place."

"Me, too! My home is way up north, cold and snowy all year round," he explained.

"What brought you to this place?" Cascadia asked.

His blue eyes sparkled as he answered. "Adventure! I wanted to see the world."

"Oh." She blinked slowly, processing that. "And you have found adventures?"

"I've had a chance to see new places and meet new people and try new things," North replied cheerily.

"I...am also doing all new things," Cascadia said, realizing they had a lot in common.

"That's magical! I think it's the best thing in the whole world," he continued. "What's your favorite thing you've done since you got to town?"

That made her pause. Cascadia thought back over the last couple of days, to all that had happened and all she had learned. It had been overwhelming but exciting, to find her kin in this place and feel like she had a home on land. But how could she explain that to him?

"Meeting my cousin," she said finally.

"Your hot chocolate, miss," interrupted David just then, setting the warm beverage in front of her.

North removed the second little candy cane from its wrapper, then paused with it over her cup. Cascadia didn't know what to expect, but she nodded anyway. Soon, the little swirl of red and white had disappeared into the dark liquid. She lifted it carefully to her lips and took a small sip.

"Oh!" Cascadia cried, pleasantly surprised.

"See? I told you, peppermint and chocolate is the perfect combination." He smiled warmly, his light blue eyes crinkling at the corners.

She took in his attractive figure, studying the way his cheekbones looked sharp against his dark blue jacket. The lighter blue underneath, likely a sweater, matched his eyes perfectly. The blonde hair she remembered from last night was brighter in the morning sun, like honey or straw, maybe.

It looked soft and Cascadia resisted the urge to reach out and run her fingers through it. Instead, she gave him her most winning smile.

"I would like to go on an adventure. You will help me?"

"Absolutely!" North leapt from his seat. "What do you like to do?"

"What is best for our first date?" Cascadia did her best to find the correct words to convey her meaning.

He hurried to finish the last of his coffee, then grabbed her hand. "Let me show you what Seaside has to offer!"

Then they were waving goodbye to David and bustling out the door of Holly Jolly Coffee, into the chilly breeze off the sea. It called to her, a soft shushing sound as the waves crashed in the distance. Her eyes automatically searched for the rushing water, the seafoam capped waves.

Cascadia fought the pull of the ocean calling her home, trying to focus instead on the warm hand holding hers as North tugged her along the pier. Up ahead, the sound of children's laughter and a soft melody filled the air, steadily growing louder. A little building with only a roof was spinning in slow circles, with small humans seated on horses.

No, not real horses, she realized. Plastic horses which bobbed and weaved as the carousel spun in its infinite loop. Twinkling lights reflected off the snow, giving the entire thing a sparkling appearance as it whirled past them.

North held out one gloved hand to her as he bowed at the waist, eyes twinkling like the lights.

"Would you join me, Miss Cascadia?"

They found a pair of horses away from the majority of the children and he helped her climb aboard. Cascadia had never ridden something like this; selkies had no concept of toys or games for entertainment's sake. Her hands gripped tightly to the pole above her horse as she tried desperately to maintain her balance.

Beside her, North spun around to ride backwards, then sideways. He seemed absolutely confident that he would not fall and injure himself. When he leaned all the way back on his horse, upside down, his hat slipped from his head. Cascadia's gaze stalled on his strangely long, pointed ears.

His laughter finally subsided as the carousel came to a crawl and eventually paused to allow new riders to join them.

"Look, daddy, it's one of Santa's elves!"

A little girl with black hair ran toward them, eyes wide. Though Cascadia had no idea what the child was talking about, the girl's father followed her closely as she approached the pair.

"I'm only on vacation for a few days," North said softly, pulling another candy cane from his pocket. "So this has to be our little secret, okay?"

"Okay!"

The child snatched the candy from his gloved hand and dashed back to her father. Cascadia looked back and forth between the two of them and her companion, trying to understand what had just happened. The words were fuzzy to her, new ones she hadn't come across before—Santa, elves, vacation.

North looked bashful as he rubbed the back of his neck. He retrieved his hat from where it had fallen and tucked it back over his pointed ears, offering her a small smile.

"I forget sometimes that I'm not at home. That I stand out here," he said.

"Where you come from, everyone has these pointy ears?" Cascadia tried to follow along.

"Yes. Can I tell you a secret?" North held her gaze.

She nodded. His tone implied that this was a big deal, something serious, though her understanding of human matters seemed to be missing several of the details. North took her hand in his again as they walked away from the carousel, out toward the beach.

"Humans think we're just a myth. Not real," he said softly. "Christmas elves, that is."

"Christmas...elves?" Cascadia tested out the words.

"At the coldest time of the year, our dear Santa brings presents to all the good boys and girls," North continued. "My family have been gift wrappers for Santa for many generations."

Images danced in her mind, faster than she could entirely make sense of them. A man in a red outfit, little people with pointy ears wearing green, Christmas decorations. Strange and unfamiliar concepts to her, all blurring together.

"It's our little secret, okay?" North winked at her.

"Our secret." Cascadia nodded. "I am also a secret. The land dwellers do not know we exist."

"Land dwellers?" His blue eyes widened in surprise.

"I come from the sea. They call my kind Selkie. We only come to land to make more selkies, then we go home," explained Cascadia to the best of her abilities.

Beside her, North coughed loudly. "To make more selkies?"

"Selkies are always girls. Only girls. We will die out on our own." Cascadia stared out at the sea as she whispered this truth to him.

Carefully, North took her hands and turned her until she faced him again. "You've come here to help your species survive?"

"Yes."

"I knew it! I heard the myths from a grumpy old fisherman the other day, and I didn't believe him that selkies were dangerous creatures here to harm people," he said firmly. "When I saw you, I think part of me just knew you were a magical being like me."

Her dark eyes closed then opened again slowly as she processed this new information. "You are not a human?"

"No. I'm an elf," North grinned, pulling his cap up on one side to flash his pointed ear.

"And I am not human. We do not belong here. You are like me." Cascadia took her time putting the words together as understanding dawned on her.

"That's right! What are the chances that we would both be here, in this little town at the edge of the sea?" He squeezed her hands firmly. "As if we were meant to find each other."

The strangest sensation filled her with those words. Warmth surged through her body and her chest squeezed. Someone like her, who did not fit in, who did not belong. Yet he felt as drawn to her as Cascadia was to him.

She did not know the human word for it, but her heart soared like a gull above the sea as she looked at the blonde elf before her. Could this be the reason she had felt the pull to land so intensely over the previous moon? Had something in him called to her, reached out through the ether, to find her?

It seemed impossible. Improbable, at best. But Cascadia had learned so much in her two days on land thus far. Her kin could and did survive among the humans, despite what they had always been told. She had family that wanted to help her with her goal of restoring the seas to ensure a future for the selkies of her pod.

Perhaps, a tiny voice whispered at the back of her mind, she had been meant to meet him, too. To live on land with Emmy and help the researchers heal the oceans. To build a life among the land dwellers by her own choice, rather than a trap set by a man who held her fur out of reach.

A life...on land. With North.

Home Away From Home

NORTH

After their unexpected heart-to-heart, North understood why he felt so at ease with Cascadia. They were both strangers in this place, magical beings that hid in plain sight among the humans. He had absolutely been drawn to her, to the otherworldliness of her beauty and the wildness in her eyes.

As they wandered down the Boardwalk hand in hand, he couldn't help the smile that stretched from ear to ear. Was this what he had been missing back home? The comfortable silence of someone who understood him on a level that no one else did?

"We should stop for ice cream," North said, gesturing to the shop up ahead. "Have you had that yet?"

Her eyes scrunched shut for a moment, then she shook her head. "No. I want to try it."

"I hope they have seasonal flavors," he commented as he led her to the pastel colored ice cream parlor in the center of the Boardwalk.

"Seasonal?" Cascadia asked.

"This time of year, when it's cold like this, certain flavors are more popular. Like the peppermint you had earlier," explained North as he held the door for her.

"Mmm! Peppermint is good," said Cascadia with a dreamy smile.

Over the shop's speakers, Christmas music played softly. A young employee stood near the glass case holding the ice cream tubs, waiting patiently for them to approach. His bored expression clashed with his mint green apron and matching hat. It made North chuckle.

He led her to the case and read off each of the flavors currently available. Cascadia listened carefully, seeming to search for the meaning of each word before nodding excitedly.

"Chocolate, vanilla, mint chocolate chip, cookies and cream, sugar cookie, peppermint swirl, marshmallow hot chocolate, and gingerbread."

The way her eyes squeezed shut as she tried to decide what to get was the cutest thing he had ever seen. North waved at the boy behind the counter to get his attention.

"Can we get a sample?" he asked politely. "My friend hasn't tried most of these flavors."

"Isn't it a little too cold out for ice cream?" asked the kid with a frown.

"It's never too cold for ice cream!" North exclaimed cheerily.

Shaking his head, the employee took a small plastic spoon from the dish and scooped a little bit of the gingerbread ice cream onto it. He reached up to hand the sample to

North, then realized that North was not tall enough to reach over the glass case to grab it. The young man looked momentarily confused, as if just realizing that the fully grown adult in front of him was considerably shorter than most people.

Without comment, North took the spoon from his hand. He turned to Cascadia, who somehow stood even shorter than him. As she took her first bite of ice cream, she let out a happy little sigh.

"This is...ginger bread?" she asked quietly.

"Yep! A popular baked good in winter." He tossed the spoon in the little trash can for her.

Cascadia's dark eyes shimmered as she replied, "I like this."

One by one, she tried each of the ice cream flavors available at the shop. While she enjoyed most of them, there was a clear winner: marshmallow hot chocolate. It seemed the selkie had a sweet tooth now that she had been introduced to chocolate. North got a scoop of peppermint swirl for himself and the hot chocolate for her.

They sat at the counter at the front of the ice cream shop, on bar stool seats facing the sea, as they ate their cold treats. North watched Cascadia's face light up every time she ate a bit more of her ice cream. When he offered her a bite of his peppermint swirl, she didn't hesitate.

"Oh! It's so sparkly." The selkie giggled. "I want that one next time. No, the gingerbread. Ah!"

"Too many choices." North laughed, understanding her trouble deciding.

They enjoyed the relative warmth of the shop as they

finished their ice cream. After tossing their trash, he led her back out into the cold, cloudy day. Cascadia shivered against the strong wind blowing in from the sea and North pulled her to his side instinctively. She seemed confused at first, but snuggled against him after a minute.

Her gloved hand fit perfectly in his, just the right size for him to give her a gentle, reassuring squeeze from time to time as they wandered. When she leaned her head against his shoulder, North couldn't help but think they were built like puzzle pieces that slotted together perfectly. While he hadn't dated very many elves back home, he was by no means inexperienced. It had never felt like this with anyone else—no matter the gender or body shape.

Cascadia shyly asked questions about his home in the North Pole and he answered them to the best of his abilities.

"What is a Santa Claus?"

"Well, the humans think he is a myth, like you and me," North spoke slowly. "He was once just a man, but his goodness and kindness became a magic all their own."

"He is like us?" she asked, looking up to meet his eyes.

"Yes, I suppose you could say he's a magical being in the same way that we are," he replied.

For hours, the two of them walked up and down the path beside the beach, talking about everything and anything. Cascadia told him about the joy of swimming beside polar bears in the icy waters north of there; North told her all about watching the baby penguins hatch each spring in the land just beyond his village.

He told her stories of growing up with his tight-knit family in theirsturdy little cottage, full of love and support. In return, she told him how magical it had been to race her sisters through warm summer waters to see who could catch the most fish. Together, they admired the setting sun as it dipped below the horizon and disappeared behind the sea.

The sudden drop in temperature seemed to startle Cascadia, who leaned further into him. North wrapped one arm around her waist and rested his cheek against the top of her head. The happiness that radiated through him felt like a living, breathing thing. Like his heart might beat right out of his chest if he were any happier.

When she tugged him toward the water, North simply followed her lead. Cascadia picked up a seashell and held it to her ear, then smiled as she offered it to him. As he held it to his ear, North could make out the sound of rushing waves.

"It is alive. A part of the sea itself," explained the selkie.

"That's amazing," he replied.

Wanting to show her a bit of his world as well, he led her toward the North Pole Bed and Breakfast. North's eyes were trained on Cascadia as they approached the happy little snow-covered house surrounded by trees. The selkie's deep brown eyes grew wide at the decorations the house boasted.

They had made it just before sunset, and she had time to admire the yards and yards of fresh green garland along the front porch and wreaths on every window. The big red bows and burlap bunting that hung from the roof added such a cozy feeling. Inside the front window, the massive Christmas tree that Ms. Eve bought sat in full view, overflowing with ornaments, ribbons, tinsel, and garland.

"This is pretty much what my village back home looks like, except we all have smaller family cottages." North took in her excitement as he spoke.

"So beautiful," Cascadia whispered.

He opened the front door for her, following her into the gorgeously decorated foyer on the little inn. Cascadia's face lit up at the additional garland, ornaments, and tinsel that covered nearly every inch of the front room. Her fingers reached carefully for a glass ornament hanging on the massive Christmas tree, taking the dolphin from its perch.

Behind her desk, Ms. Eve raised both of her white eyebrows at him. North offered her a lopsided grin as he helped the selkie place the ornament back where it belonged. He reached behind her to secure it just a bit higher than she could comfortably reach on her own, and savored the feeling of her warm body pressed close to his.

"Welcome home, Mr. Snowstorm," called Ms. Eve loudly. "I see you've brought a friend."

Cascadia whirled around, trying to find the source of the voice. When the old woman climbed down from her chair and walked over to introduce herself, the selkie's shoulders relaxed. It was clear from her height and those pointed ears that she was a Christmas elf like North, and therefore no threat to the girl.

"I'm Ms. Eve. Welcome to my humble little home away from home."

"Nice to meet you," answered Cascadia with a small smile. "I come from the sea. I wish to see North's home. It is lovely!"

"From the sea, hmm?" Ms. Eve's eyes slid to North's and he shrugged.

"You've been here long enough to know the stories," said North simply.

The old woman scanned his selkie from head to toe, taking in every detail. "Indeed I have, young man."

With that, she padded softly back to her desk and hopped into her high-backed chair. Cascadia seemed completely unbothered by the woman and her knowing the selkie's secret, so North decided it would be fine. They chatted on a settee beside the roaring fire in the front room and warmed themselves from their day spent outdoors.

It didn't take long for Ms. Eve to appear beside them, a cup of milk and a plate of cookies in her hands. On the gold rimmed dish sat two gingerbread men, two snickerdoodle cookies, two chocolate cookies with peppermint bits, and something dipped in chocolate. North picked one up and examined it, trying to guess what was inside.

"Those are a local favorite," Ms. Eve informed him. "Ritz crackers with creamy peanut butter, dipped in dark chocolate. They stay crisp in the freezer till the end of the season."

"That sounds magical." North immediately bit into the cookie and his eyes rolled back in pleasure.

He took his time teaching Cascadia about all the different types of Christmas cookies. She tried them one by one, always pausing to savor the flavors that were brand new to her. North held up the gingerbread men, handing one to the selkie. They each bit off one leg and enjoyed the crisp snap of the perfectly baked cookies.

Then North showed her how to dip the sturdier cookie into the milk for several long seconds to soften it. When she held hers in the liquid for too long and it crumbled, she looked genuinely confused.

"It's alright, that happens sometimes." He dipped his cookie again and offered it to her. "There's a very fine line between soft and soaked."

Warm blankets and creamy hot cocoa by the fire had

them feeling considerably better in no time. Cascadia had insisted that North put one of his miniature candy canes in her cocoa and the content sigh that slipped from her lips made him blush.

Truly, he thought he could watch her adorable and honest reactions to all the human world had to offer forever.

Magical

CASCADIA

As Cascadia finished off the last of her cookies and hot chocolate, she snuggled closer to North. His strong shoulders and bright eyes brought her the strangest sense of comfort, like she belonged there. Her dark hair cascaded over her shoulders, mostly crushed between their bodies, but he didn't seem to mind.

Their conversation meandered slowly through a variety of topics before he asked if he could walk her home. She tilted her head at him inquisitively.

"It's considered a gentleman's responsibility to make sure the lady gets home safe after a date," said North.

"Oh," she gasped. "Does that make me a lady? I thought I was a magical creature."

A rumbling belly laugh escaped him at that and she couldn't help but giggle, too. When their laughter subsided, he led her to the front door of the bed and breakfast. North helped her put her coat and gloves back on, then dressed himself for the chilly weather. Ms. Eve called out a greeting as they stepped out the door.

From a few steps off the front porch, she turned to look back at the pretty little house. Hundreds of little sparkling lights danced along every edge of the building, down the bannisters and along the porch railing. Every bit of the greenery from earlier glowed now with the warm, soft light of the little bulbs and the sight took her breath away.

"Wow," Cascadia whispered.

"Isn't it stunning?" North grinned at her.

"Like swimming with a thousand baby jellyfish," she said softly, remembering the nearest experience she had had under the sea.

"That sounds absolutely magical," replied North excitedly. "I wish I could see that someday."

Together, they made the long, slow walk back across town. Cascadia's sense of direction on land was not great, but she knew to keep the sea to her left to get back to Emmy and her grandmother's house. North followed her lead, in no rush to get her back to her kin.

When the little cabin came into sight, Cascadia paused. Her heart beat a steady rhythm in her chest and she realized that she had hardly thought about how to work her human legs or her lungs throughout their busy day. She had been so consumed with North's attention and his company that there had been no time to worry about such trivial things.

Only a couple of days ago, she had struggled with such basic functions on land. It was becoming clear to her how easily she could adjust to this life, as Marissa had. Cascadia would not struggle nearly as much as she had initially assumed, if she stayed on land with Emmy and her grandmother and this handsome blonde elf.

The thought should have caused panic to race through her veins, but instead, she felt strangely hopeful. Cascadia tilted her chin up to look into North's icy blue eyes and bit her bottom lip, suddenly bashful.

"May I kiss you, Cascadia?" he asked sweetly.

She managed a nod, unsure of her voice in that moment. The longing in his eyes seemed to match her own. When North placed one gloved hand on her cheek and the other under her chin, she followed his lead. Cascadia stretched up on her tiptoes and leaned her head back, giving him better access to her mouth.

For a long, slow, perfect eternity, they kissed. His warm hands against her cold cheeks felt lovely; nearly as good as his warm breath against her face and his lips against hers. It took Cascadia several moments to come back to her body after the marvelous floating feeling those kisses had elicited from her.

"I had a wonderful time with you today," whispered North in a deeper, huskier voice than she was used to. "Please tell me I can see you again tomorrow."

"Yes," Cascadia breathed out, her mouth only inches from his.

"I know you have plans, things to attend to while you're visiting. But it would be my absolute pleasure to spend as much of the remaining time with you as possible." He kissed her cheek between words.

Her face felt terribly warm, but she returned his smile. "I would like that very much."

"Good." North took both of her hands in his. "I don't

think I've ever liked someone this much, Cascadia. I can't wait to see you tomorrow."

They shared another long, languid kiss in the snowy light of the moon. Words were hard for Cascadia to put together as she stared dreamily into those blue, blue eyes. All sense of cold had disappeared and the worries of this morning seemed to fade away when North looked at her like that.

He bid her goodnight and watched until she stepped into the cabin. The heater felt sweltering to her in that moment, flushed from his kisses and wearing entirely too many layers. Cascadia hurriedly pulled off her winter coat and hung it beside Emmy's. She kicked off her boots and tucked her gloves back into the jacket pocket, but still felt far too hot.

"I know that look all too well." Marissa chuckled from her seat on the couch, where she and Emmy were snuggled under a blanket watching a movie.

"The date was good?" Emmy asked, hopping up. "How was he? Is he as charming and kind as he is handsome? Tell me everything!"

Embarrassed, Cascadia ducked her head to hide her scarlet cheeks. "It was...magical."

"Ah, someone is smitten, I see," commented the old woman.

Emmy pulled her down on the couch between them and demanded a recounting of the entire day, from start to finish. As Cascadia told them about all the fun she had and all the new things she had tried, the girl made happy little sounds to encourage her to keep talking. She focused on her cousin, rather than the elder to her left, as she described the sight of the inn with its countless sparkling lights as they walked away.

For longer than she realized, she recounted every detail of her very first date to Emmy there on her worn couch. Soon, both girls began to yawn. With a knowing smile, the old woman told them they could talk more in the morning. Then she shooed Emmy off to her bedroom and tucked a knitted blanket around Cascadia's feet, sides, and shoulders.

"What an eventful day, little one," Marissa said softly. "Sleep now. There will be more adventures when you wake."

Then the darkness of sleep overtook her and Cascadia faded into a dreamless rest.

As Far As Anyone Else Knows

NORTH

In the morning, North got dressed for the day and headed downstairs to the front room. Ms. Eve greeted him with a little wave. She hopped down from her high-backed chair and walked the few steps to him, a sealed letter in her hand. The letter was addressed to him, at this location, in Oregon.

With deft fingers, he tore open the envelope and held the letter up to read it. His parents had written to tell him how much they missed him. That they wished he would come home, now that he had had his taste of the world beyond the North Pole.

North sighed. The handful of days he had gotten to experience beyond his home were nowhere near enough to satisfy his curiosity. In fact, he had more questions than ever. And a longer to do list. He wanted to take his pretty selkie to every place in town, to show her what a life on land could look like.

Underneath his parents' words was a note from his

brother, West. As the eldest, he felt he had the right to tell North what to do. Usually, his advice was welcome and often even helpful. But in this case, his wanderlust was beyond his brother's capability to understand.

He knew his brother had the best of intentions. Neither of them liked to see their mother upset and they would do nearly anything to prevent such a circumstance. This, though—this was not something North could just give up. Mrs. Claus had promised him one month away from their home in the North Pole, and he refused to waste even a moment of it.

As soon as he folded the letter and tucked it into his pocket, the proprietor of the establishment turned back to look at him.

"Letter from home?" she asked, though he knew she was well aware.

"They miss me." North gave an exaggerated sigh. "They want me to cut my trip early."

"After all the trouble Lady Christmas went through to get you here?" Ms. Eve looked surprised.

North rubbed one hand across the back of his neck, flustered. "It feels ungrateful to just give it all up. It's everything I've ever wanted."

"Best stay and finish out your adventure, then," the old woman said.

Though her tone came off as chiding, he felt relieved to hear his own thoughts reflected back to him. It had taken all of his courage to request this opportunity. He couldn't simply give it all up, no matter how much he missed his family.

With a frown, she turned that steady gaze on him.

"Have you considered staying, my boy?"

"Staying? Here?" North could barely whisper the words aloud. "What would I even do?"

"Well, I've been running this place on my own for a very long time, you know," Ms. Eve informed him. "Some day in the near future, I will no longer be able to do so. It would be such a shame to close down the bed and breakfast after all these years."

His blue eyes widened at that. "You...need help?"

"Help, most assuredly. A successor eventually," the woman said confidently.

"I...had never considered such a thing," North admitted, biting his lower lip.

"Did you know that this place has been open for nearly two hundred years?" added Ms. Eve. "I'm the second owner. And despite the long lives we elves enjoy, I am finding it harder to manage lately."

The idea took root in him instantly. North could picture himself carrying bags up to rooms for guests and offering recommendations for where to get dinner. Becoming part of the community in this small town at the edge of the sea. He imagined himself booking reservations and hosting magical creatures from across the globe in search of somewhere new.

Maybe it would amount to nothing, in the end. But the thought of it brought a wide grin to his face and Ms. Eve returned it. A thought occurred to him and North turned back to her.

"Are there any other guests staying here at the moment?"

"Hmm? Oh, we'll get a few people on December first," the old woman replied.

"Can I ask..." North hesitated, not wanting to be rude.

"How does this bed and breakfast stay open with so few guests?"

"We provide a necessary service to all magical beings. This place is one of a handful of locations across the globe that is managed for the good of all," Ms. Eve explained simply.

Though North still had many questions, he let the topic drop. He could get more information later. For now, all he wanted to do was go find Cascadia. The curvaceous selkie appeared in his mind, all long dark hair and soft, tan skin. And those eyes. Like liquid chocolate, dark and deep and soulful.

With Ms. Eve's help, he had decided where to take her for their second date. He had been hesitant to the suggestion at first, but North allowed the older elf to convince him. The aquarium would allow him a glimpse into Cascadia's life in the sea and might possibly even make her feel less homesick.

He bundled up in his winter gear and headed back to the Boardwalk, where he hoped to find Cascadia. When he arrived at Holly Jolly Coffee, his eyes immediately fell on the beautiful woman waiting for him. North's heart beat faster as he stepped inside and she turned to look at him.

"Good morning, Cascadia," he said brightly.

"Good morning, North," she replied, her smile shy.

"I have a surprise planned for you today," North continued. "Shall we?"

He held out his arm and the selkie blinked at him for a moment. North whispered that she should take his arm in hers so they could walk together to their date location.

Cascadia's dark eyes crinkled as she grinned at him, following his instructions.

"Now we look like a human couple!" she cried happily.

"As far as anyone else knows, we are." North tossed her a saucy wink.

Cascadia's delighted little squeal at that warmed his heart. While he had been on plenty of dates back in the North Pole, none had made him as giddy as this one. Maybe it was because she wasn't an elf that he had grown up with all his life, or maybe it was because everything was new to her.

All North Snowstorm knew in that moment was that he would very much like to spend the rest of his days arm in arm with this dark-haired beauty. The warmth of her side pressed into his as they walked the short distance to the Seaside Aquarium.

Her curves fitted against him in all the right places when they fell into step. Those lush hips he had been itching to get his hands on bumped his with every other step and North tried not to let his mind wander. There would be time for that later.

At the entrance to the aquarium, he pulled out the dollar bills that Mrs. Claus had gave him for his trip. North paid the woman at the counter for two day passes and led Cascadia into the slightly warmer building, one hand on her middle back as he guided her through the crowd.

They stepped to the side of the front hall and removed their coats. The sight of Cascadia in a fitted blue sweater dress that hugged her every curve nearly undid him then and there. If North walked behind her half a step, he could watch that round bottom bounce with every move.

He shook his head, trying to focus. But when she slipped her soft hand into his and looked up at him through those full, dark lashes, North forgot how to breathe. This stunning woman might just be the death of him.

"Over there, we can watch the Harbor Seals." He cleared his throat, cheeks bright pink. "I thought you might like that. They're...like cousins to you, right?"

Cascadia's molten brown eyes went hazy for a moment, as if she was thinking hard about what he had said. "Yes. That is close enough."

"Will you show me? What the world looks like from that point of view?" North asked softly.

With a giggle, she tugged on his arm and pulled him toward the seal habitat. Cascadia pressed against the glass, her fingers spread wide and her nose at risk of being squished. As if sensing her, several of the seals in the enclosure turned their way.

One, with a pale belly and grey spots, swam languidly toward her. For several moments, the seal simply stared at Cascadia while it swam by. Then it turned in a quick loop and came back for another look at her.

Perfectly still, barely breathing, his selkie tilted her head to one side. The seal seemed to recognize the animal-like gesture. He blinked twice, slow and sure, before racing off to rejoin his friends. The others took a while longer to approach, but eventually they each took their turn inspecting her with unbridled curiosity.

"They recognize me," whispered Cascadia.

"These seals were born and raised in this aquarium." North pointed to a sign as he read it aloud.

"No, no. Not from the sea. They recognize me as a cousin.

As one of them," she said, eyes still locked on the graceful creatures gliding through the water.

He could have watched her forever, the way she seemed to speak to the seals through the glass with only her eyes and body language. The sheer joy emitting from every inch of her body felt contagious, bathing him in a fidgety excitement he couldn't explain. It took all of North's strength to pull her from the viewing area, toward the seal feeding station.

Out of the corner of his eye, he saw the Harbor seals follow them to the other section of their enclosure. North showed Cascadia the area where they could buy shrimp and small fish to feed to the seals and quickly bought several. As she stepped toward the opening and bent at the waist to offer the first fish to a seal, the white-bellied one from earlier rushed to meet her.

North simply watched in awe as his beautiful selkie took turns feeding and petting each of the seals in turn. Every time she turned those pleading brown eyes on him, he bought more fish. There could be no denying that sweet smile. He melted completely at the sight.

You'll Come Back to Us?

CASCADIA

The tickle of the seal's fur soothed something inside of Cascadia. She locked eyes with the creature as North handed her another cold shrimp. Understanding passed through those dark, watery brown eyes as she watched her distant cousin happily snatch the snack from her hand.

It was strange to think that she could easily have been in its place, held captive on land with no way to return to the sea. Cascadia wondered how often Emmy's gran, Marissa, had visited these seals over the years of her captivity. If she had brought her daughter, and then her granddaughter, to play with their kin like this.

If she stayed on land, would this be the closest she would get to her home and her pod from now on? Perhaps she could hold onto her magic, changing forms from time to time. Certainly, she would have the opportunity which had not been afforded to any who came before her.

Marissa would safeguard her fur when she walked on two legs. Surely the elder would continue to look after her and any younger selkies who dared to transform in their search for love and children. Would North be okay with her diving back into the sea? Cascadia wondered if he would be the type of partner who supported her choices, or if he would feel the risk was too high.

If she had children on land, like Marissa had, would she ever dare to leave them to go see her sisters? Or would she go back to the sea to have her child, that they might be creatures of the water, too? Her thoughts swirled as she tried to imagine what that future might feel like.

A headache began to throb at the back of her skull. These were not decisions she could make lightly. The plans, the expectations, that she had come to land with no longer held true for Cascadia. While the elders she had grown up with had not purposely lied to her, there were many things they did not know or understand.

"Should we go see the other exhibits?" North asked, placing one hand on her shoulder.

Cascadia tilted her head so she could look up at him. "What else is there to see?"

"There are octopus and wolf eels in the next room," he said, pointing to a sign.

"Oh! Octopus are very clever," Cascadia replied, perking up.

For hours, the two of them wandered ever so slowly around the entirety of the aquarium. They took their time with each sea creature. She wanted to reach out and touch each of them, as she had with the seals in the feeding area. To let them know that she was there, and though she looked like a human, she was truly one of them.

North made sure they stopped for lunch, which had

been the furthest thing from Cacadia's mind as she surrounded herself with the familiar sights and sounds of her home. By the time the aquarium closed, they had done at least three full laps of the building. His warm hand in hers gave Cascadia the most soothing feeling of being safe with him.

"I think that I could go anywhere and have a good time as long as you're with me," the elf told her. "Someday, I hope to go snorkeling so you can really show me your home."

"Snorkeling? I do not know this word," Cascadia hesitated.

"I can bring a tank of oxygen, allowing me to breathe for a long time under the sea," North explained patiently.

"Truly? That would be—magical!" she gasped.

The smile that broke across her face must have been contagious, because North's face split wide in a grin as well. As he walked her back to Emmy's cabin, he told her more stories about his life back home in the frozen north. Cascadia listened attentively, absorbing as much as she could, trying to imagine a place that was somehow land but also frozen water all year round.

By the time they reached the cozy little A-frame covered in snow, its chimney billowing, her ears were freezing and her nose ached from the cold. North had held her left hand for about half of the walk, then switched sides to warm her other hand the rest of the way. His kindness and thoughtfulness were so different from the stories she had heard all her life about men.

Perhaps it was his elvish nature, or where he had grown up. Either way, Cascadia found it endlessly charming. To be treated with such sweetness, to be doted on, to see the adoration in his blue eyes every time he looked at her. The selkie had never imagined such a relationship in her wildest dreams.

"Can I see you tomorrow?" North gazed dreamily down at her, making her blush.

"Yes. I would like it very much," answered Cascadia without hesitation. "I will wait at the Holly Jolly Coffee for you once I am available."

Then she leaned up onto her tiptoes to place a soft kiss on his lips. A moment later, North's strong arms were wrapped around her waist and his mouth was on hers. Cascadia reveled in the giddy, electric feeling of kissing him. She had never felt anything like it in all her moons.

With a sigh, he eventually pulled away. His hands lingered on her hips, though, as if he truly could not bear to be separated from her.

"I will find you there, my darling girl," North whispered in her ear.

"Goodnight," Cascadia whispered back.

When she stepped into the cabin, the selkie leaned against the closed door, her head falling back as her eyes closed. What was this feeling? This joy, this excitement, every time she looked at him. The elders had explained attraction and how to woo a man to make more selkies, but this was something else, Cascadia was certain.

At the dining table, two pairs of curious eyes were trained on her. Her face flushed as she remembered that they shared this small space. Emmy hopped up to prepare her a plate and Cascadia sat down to join them.

"Fresh-caught sturgeon with garlic butter pasta and

veggies," Marissa informed her, pausing as she processed the new words.

"Oh. It's good!" she said, immediately reaching for another bite.

After dinner, Emmy tells her that she has good news. "You got an interview with the conservation team!"

"What does this mean?" Cascadia asked, trying to keep her voice steady.

"You will dress nicely and speak to someone in charge about working there," said Marissa. "As long as that goes well, they will offer you a job. You'll be able to do what you came here to do."

"Truly?" The selkie fought back tears.

Beside her, the red-headed girl took her hands and jumped up and down. "You've totally got this, Cascadia! We'll get you ready for your interview."

"Thank you, cousin," she managed, her voice choking with emotion.

After a brief discussion with Marissa, they decided it would be best for Cascadia to return to the sea to tell the others of her plan and progress. Much had changed in the few days since she had arrived on land and they would be worried if they did not hear from her soon. Her heart soared at the chance to transform to her true self and see her sisters.

But a small new part of her heart squeezed tight at the thought of leaving Emmy, Marissa, and North. Cascadia wondered at that; she had only known them for such a short time. Yet her feelings for the three of them felt just as important as her love for her sisters and her pod.

Still, she had her obligations. They decided that she would leave before sunrise the next day, slipping away in the dark of night with no one to notice her. It made Cascadia smile, the way that Marissa still knew to consider such things and hide her true nature from the land dwellers.

When the moon hung high and bright in the sky, the three women walked out of the woods and onto the nearest slip of beach. The sand slid under Cascadia's bare feet as she handed her shoes and socks to Emmy. Then she slipped out of her dress. Marissa handed her the fur she had arrived in, knowing it would not be possible to transform without it.

"You'll come back to us?" whispered a tearful Emmy. "You promise?"

The selkie took her cousin's hands in hers. "I will be back soon."

"Give everyone our love, child," said the old woman, voice wavering.

Cascadia slipped into the icy waves, the cold biting at her soft human flesh in ways it never had in her true form. She willed herself back to her natural state, her body shifting and twisting painfully as she transformed. When her warm fur surrounded every inch of her body, the selkie paused in wonder.

Immediately, the sea felt less frigid. The layers of blubber and fur made all the difference as she settled her bones back into their original places. It all felt familiar like a dream, rather than something actively happening to Cascadia at that moment. Her mind raced, switching between her seal instincts and her more human awareness.

Hesitantly, she poked her head just above the surface. Emmy and her grandmother stood side by side on the beach, waving goodbye to her. They both stifled sobs behind their winter coats and Cascadia found it hard to leave them like that.

Tinsel & Balsam

NORTH

The next morning, North Snowstorm slept in late. He took a leisurely, steamy shower in the large standing shower attached to his room at the bed and breakfast. After, he found himself singing the lyrics to You Make It Feel Like Christmas to himself as he towel-dried his hair.

"I want to thank the storm that brought the snow," he sang loudly into the empty room. "Thanks to the string of lights that make it glow. I want to thank you, baby."

By the time he made it downstairs, Ms. Eve drawled,"I thought you might sleep the whole day away, young man."

Her snarkiness didn't bother him in the slightest, though. North had a date with a beautiful girl and another magical, adventurous, exciting day in Seaside ahead of him. Nothing could possibly ruin his good mood. When the older elf disappeared for a few minutes and returned with a warm cinnamon roll and two sausage links, he smiled.

North took the plate to the living room and tucked into it

while Ms. Eve puttered about behind her desk. Soon she appeared in front of him, a cup of steaming coffee in hand.

"I thought you might like to try the hazelnut cappuccino today."

"That sounds delicious," he said, taking a long sniff. "Mmm!"

He sipped slowly on the hot coffee, enjoying the chocolatey undertones of the drink. Out the front window, he watched the snow fall. Snowflakes danced in the air before settling on the snow-covered ground in front of the bed and breakfast.

The sound of waves crashing in the distance grew louder as a family of elves stepped through the front door. A young couple with small children attempted to wrangle all of their luggage into the building without tripping. North watched as the little elves took off to explore the new place, their parents calling after them to settle down.

"Welcome to the North Pole Bed and Breakfast," Ms. Eve announced as she stood.

"Thank you! As you can see, we're very excited for our first trip away from home," said the pretty, petite blonde elf with green eyes.

"Apologies in advance for their rowdiness," her wife added, staring after the two smallest elves. "I hope we won't disturb the rest of your guests too much."

North held out a hand to her, admiring the sharp cheekbones and hint of strawberry in her blonde locks. When she shook his hand, her grip felt steady and firm in his.

"I'm Finley Wintershire. This is my wife, Ivy," said the taller elf.

"And the energetic little elves over there are Tinsel and Balsam," Ivy added with a fond smile.

"As it turns out, North Snowstorm here is our only other guest at the moment," Ms. Eve informed them kindly, gesturing to him.

North smiled brightly at them. "No bother at all!"

"That's a relief," replied Ivy, watching her little ones out of the corner of her eye.

At that, Ms. Eve insisted on checking the family in and showing them to their adjoining rooms. She gathered their room keys, taking the bags from Ivy curtly. It seemed like the perfect opportunity for North to slip out and go find his pretty selkie. But as he placed his hand on the doorknob, coat in hand, a cry and a crash sounded from the stairs.

Immediately, he sprinted to check on everyone. Ivy stood at the top of the stairway, both hands over her mouth, with the children clinging to her legs. Halfway down the stairs, Finley held Ms. Eve in both arms, her steady grip the only reason the older woman hadn't tumbled headfirst to the landing.

"Is everyone alright?" North shouted.

"Just a sprained ankle, my dears," called back Ms. Eve, loud enough for everyone to hear. "I'll be fine. I'm tougher than I look."

The grimace on her face when Finley helped her to her feet said otherwise, though. North hurried up the stairs to her other side and together they got her safely back onto the first floor. He insisted she get comfortable on the couch by the fire and put her leg up while he got some ice for her ankle.

Surprisingly, the older woman didn't protest. That

worried North quite a bit, so he asked the tall elf to watch over her while he got what they needed from the kitchen. Meanwhile, Ivy and the children gathered their bags and put everything into the rooms. He could hear her giving them gentle, reassuring instructions.

"We will go down and check on her once everything is put away," Ivy's sweet voice echoed through the open doorway. "Mom will take good care of her while we do this."

Drawers opened and closed upstairs as North found the ice packs and kitchen towels he wanted to ease the swelling on Ms. Eve's ankle. Back in the front room, Finley inspected the damage with the softest of touches on the sore spot.

"I'm afraid it's rather likely that it's broken, Ms. Eve," the elf said quietly.

"Oh, nonsense!" cried the old woman, waving her away. "I suppose I ought to stay off it for the rest of the day, though?"

Her knowing gaze turned to North. As if she had spoken the words aloud, he knew exactly what she expected of him.

"I can manage the front desk for you," said North without hesitation.

The next thing he knew, she was shouting orders and instructions for the various programs on her computer. North hurriedly scribbled notes in a yellow notepad, trying to keep track of all the little details. Passwords, programs, phone greetings, the list seemed to go on forever. His head spun with all the new information.

And so North found himself working at the North Pole Bed and Breakfast for the first time.

It Always Ends the Same

CASCADIA

By the time the sun crested over the waves and its light filtered through the sea, Cascadia could see the underwater caverns that her pod had called home for many generations. Her younger sister Ellery waited at the mouth of the cave entrance, on guard duty. When she caught sight of Cascadia, her eyes grew wide.

"Sister!" Ellery called, throwing herself at her.

"I am safe, little one," replied Cascadia as they embraced. "I have much to tell you. Can you gather the others?"

"You'll stay here and guard the entrance?" asked the younger selkie.

Cascadia nodded and that was enough for her sister, who swam off in search of the rest of their pod. Her liquid brown eyes took in every bit of the scene around her—the fish swimming past, the coral and kelp off to her left, and the sound of a boat far above them. As if seeing it all for the first time, she couldn't help but marvel at the beauty she found.

A fever of stingrays glided past, their dark bodies

swirling and turning with the tide. The sight felt majestic, after her days on land with no access to the sea she had always known. Someone tackled her from behind, causing Cascadia to tumble through the waves head over fins.

"You're home!" Nerissa cried, joy clear in her dark eyes.

"This will always be my home," she said.

The two touched foreheads for a long moment, reassuring each other that all was well. Then her little sister nudged her along toward their main cavern, a half-submerged space with room for the entire pod. Some of the selkies reclined on the rocks around the rim of the cave while others floated lazily in the pool at the center.

At the top of the cavernous space, a hole allowed the sunlight to filter in and brightened the space. Cascadia took in the sight of the several dozen selkies she had grown up with; her mother, her elders, her sisters, and the rest of their kin. A low hum of excitement vibrated through the space as they noticed her.

"Daughter of mine," her mother whispered into her ear as they embraced. "Thank the stars you are home and unharmed."

"I have missed you. But I come bearing news that cannot wait," said Cascadia.

Her mother clapped both fins together and the room settled into silence, except for the lapping of the waves against the cave walls.

"Your attention, please."

"There is much we don't know about the humans," Cascadia began. "But we do know that they are damaging our waters and making life harder for every living creature below the sea."

A murmur of agreement worked its way through the assembly of selkies. Many shook their heads, unhappy with the truth of their current situation.

"I come bearing much news. First, that our departed elder Nerissa who disappeared many moons ago has been on land all this time," she continued, pausing to let the others process this.

Her mother's gasp echoed through the cave. "She's alive?"

"She fell in love with a human man and had a daughter on land," explained Cascadia. "When he died unexpectedly of a human illness, she stayed to raise her daughter. That daughter grew up healthy and happy and fell in love, too."

The small space practically hummed with emotion as they all took in those words. What it meant to have a daughter on land. How she could not have abandoned the girl for anything in all the seas. Questions were whispered, low and uncertain, between selkies.

"To her great sadness, her daughter died in childbirth with her firstborn. Leaving Nerissa to raise her grandchild on her own as well," she continued.

After some time for everyone to react to that news, Cascadia filled the others in on the name-change and what Marissa had been up to all these years. She explained about knowing she couldn't go home, about infusing her magic into the tea. How it had bestowed her knowledge on Cascadia with a single cup.

Disbelief filled many of the faces looking back at her. Fear of the land dwellers and their world had been long ingrained into selkie culture, and for good reason. Just because Nerissa had found a truly good man didn't make it likely that others would be able to do the same. She understood the doubts that plagued her kin.

"It is a lot of new information, I know," Cascadia kept her voice steady. "But with Marissa's help, with her magic, we can safely navigate the land and find mates to repopulate our pod."

"Then you're home for good?" Ellery asked, eyes bright.

She shook her head sadly. "No, starfish. I must go back to work with the humans who are trying to repair the damage done to our seas. We know much that they do not. My help will improve their success, which will benefit all creatures of the sea."

"Why must you do this, Cascadia?" her mother demanded.

"Someone must do it, mother." The selkie sighed. "I feel a connection to Marissa, who remembers me from when I was small, and her granddaughter. Our cousin. I can do so much good for our pod from there."

Nerissa, the youngest of the three, rushed forward. "Are you sure that's all that it is? Or have you gone and fallen in love with a human man as well, and now you want to turn your back on your kin?"

"It isn't like that." Cascadia's face fell.

"I don't believe you," pouted Ellery, sidling up beside Nerissa.

Their mother shook her head vehemently. "I will not accept this. Let someone else go in your place. You know that men cannot be trusted. He will break your heart and leave when he has had his fill of you. They always do."

"North isn't like that," whispered Cascadia. "He isn't even

a human! He is something else. An elf, from the land that is always frozen."

"Nonsense!" cried her mother.

"We know nothing about such creatures," said a selkie behind them.

Another voice chimed in, "How can we possibly trust him?"

"You will see, Cascadia. It always ends the same."

"Enjoy your dalliance with him, then return to the sea," her sisters begged.

Her heart ached at the thought of never seeing North again. His kind eyes, that charming smile, the gentle way he kissed her. As if she was a treat that he couldn't get enough of. No, Cascadia could not stay with her pod. She would not abandon him without a word.

And she knew, deep down inside, that if she returned to her elf, her fate would be sealed. She would not give him up. If they had a child, Cascadia could never stand to leave them to go home. The possibility of that magical, happy future filled her with a new joy.

A life she had never imagined for herself, but now desperately wanted to create.

Staying in Seaside

NORTH

While running the North Pole Bed and Breakfast seemed easy enough, North found himself rushing to and fro for the rest of the day. Ms. Eve made a schedule and a to do list and kept to it strictly. By the time dinner had been served and cleaned up for the six of them, North only wanted to collapse into his bed.

Instead, he helped the proprietor to her quarters, which were thankfully located on the first floor. She had a little apartment at the back and assured him that she would be alright on her own for the night. He hesitated to leave her, but she insisted.

"Off to bed with you, young Snowstorm," chided Ms. Eve. "There will be plenty more work to do tomorrow. Get some rest while you can."

Obeying her command, North headed up to his own room. He took a long, steamy shower and stretched his sore muscles. This type of work differed from his gift-wrapping job substantially. There were so many things to keep track of, tasks to juggle, and priorities to remember.

Though he was exhausted, his mind buzzed with all the information he had learned that day. All the different parts involved in running this place, keeping it tidy, looking after each guest personally. It had been exhilarating, truth be told.

North wanted to tell his family about his day. He wished he could tell his mother about the meal Ms. Eve had talked him through making for everyone, about cooking the fresh fish she had picked up just the day before. His father would love the way he had used the handyman skills he had taught both boys to make small repairs around the place.

Briefly, he wondered if it would be possible for them to visit him there in Oregon. If North stayed to look after the bed and breakfast, would his family come to see him? Or would they feel betrayed that he decided to leave behind the life they had built for him?

Sleep pulled him under as those thoughts circled around in his mind. When he got up extra early the next morning, North hurried downstairs to check on Ms. Eve. He knocked softly on the door to her rooms and waited.

"Good morning! It's North, just checking on you."

"Good morning to you, young Snowstorm," called the older woman. "Come on in. I'm up and ready for the day. We have work to do!"

He chuckled at that. "Indeed we do. I'm at your service, Ms. Eve."

For several hours, she kept him running around the bed and breakfast with nonstop tasks. It seemed she had been managing everything by herself for entirely too long, with projects stacking up as she struggled to do more manual things. North ran one hand through his blonde hair, ruffling it as the older elf showed him the steps for making a reservation for the second time.

While he had the basics down, he always seemed to miss one step or another along the process. It would take North some practice to get the hang of it. He felt confident that he would get it by the end of the week, with a little patience and coaching from Ms. Eve.

By the time he settled in at the desk for his lunch break, North felt like he had accomplished more in the last two days than he had in a month of gift-wrapping back home. The presents needed to be wrapped, of course. It was important work.

But to him, it felt impersonal. A sticker with the name of the child and "from Santa" went in the bottom left corner of each and every gift the elves wrapped. Most objects were placed in cardboard boxes, creating a smooth cube to wrap. Rinse and repeat.

North had been endlessly bored for the last couple of years, repeating the same perfect corner folds over and over. After just two days of helping to manage the North Pole Bed and Breakfast, he felt more invigorated than he had in too long. The only problem now was getting in touch with Cascadia to explain why he hadn't been able to meet her yesterday as planned.

He dialed the number for Holly Jolly Coffee and waited as it rang a few times before someone picked up.

"Holly Jolly Coffee, how can I help you today?" asked David from the other end of the phone.

"David! This is North. The...um, pointy eared fella you made coffee for the other day," the elf struggled to find the right words. "You know Emmy, right? I'm trying to get in touch with her cousin, Cascadia."

A brief pause made North second guess himself, but then David answered. "Oh, yeah, hey man. I can send Emmy a message and give her your number, if that works for you."

"Magical! I mean, um, wonderful!" North cried. "Thanks so much, buddy."

After a few minutes, David read back the phone number for the bed and breakfast to confirm it. North nodded, forgetting the other man could not see him, and thanked him again for his help. Since he would be tied up here for the next few days, it would be better if Cascadia came over to spend time with him.

Though he was disappointed that he wouldn't be able to take her on another date as soon as he'd have liked, North couldn't help the grin that spread across his face at the thought of seeing her again soon. He pictured her face in his mind—soft tan skin, dark eyes, flowing waves of dark brown hair. His selkie.

"What's got you smiling like that, young Snowstorm?" Ms. Eve asked loudly from where she rested with her leg up.

"I enjoy this work far more than I expected," North admitted. "And I think—that is, if you want me to stick around, I should very much like to stay on here."

The older elf raised one white eyebrow, smirking at him. "It has nothing at all to do with that pretty young woman you brought home the other night?"

"W-well, of course, I like Cascadia." He blushed furiously.

"Of course I would love for you to stay on at the North Pole Bed and Breakfast, you silly boy." Ms. Eve chuckled good-naturedly. "It would be a blessed relief for these old bones. You have the energy, the stamina, to do all the major tasks."

"What would you do?" North asked, suddenly realizing he might sound like he was trying to replace the old woman.

"Oh, don't you worry about me, young man. I can do paperwork and supply ordering and the other behind-the-scenes tasks that will take longer for you to learn," replied Ms. Eve.

His heart soared. Could all his wildest dreams really be coming true? It had seemed impossible mere weeks ago. Seeing the human world for a little while, hoping the memories would tide him for the rest of his days, had been the most he ever hoped for.

But this magical place already felt like home to North and he loved the way the days seemed to stretch out before him as he thought of his new life. A joyous laugh bubbled out of him as he squeezed his eyes shut and concentrated on the happiness filling his entire body. He would have a job he adored helping others and the support of a kindly mentor.

If all went well when he got his chance to explain everything to Cascadia, North just might find himself truly living a Christmas fairytale. He couldn't wait to tell her about his plans. To make plans with Cascadia, for their future.

The hazy daydream of a future beside the gorgeous selkie appeared in his mind. A little cottage of their own, daily walks on the beach, Christmas in snowy Oregon every winter. Maybe even a little one running around someday, with her dark hair and his bright eyes.

North could practically see it now: him lifting a little girl up to feed the otters, Cascadia luring all the creatures closer.

Snow falling outside while the fire roared in their fireplace, mugs of hot cocoa in hand. It was nearly the life he had grown up knowing.

But North had never felt the way he did about his selkie with any of the elves back home. No one had ever made his heart beat this way, his insides turn to mush. Her curiosity for the human world made her irresistible, the way she found such joy in all the new experiences they had. Perhaps together, they could build a beautiful life with the best of both their homes.

The phone rang and startled him from his daydreaming.

"North Pole Bed and Breakfast, how can I help you today?" North answered quickly.

"Oh, good, I got you!" Emmy's voice echoed a bit. "We got your message. Cascadia missed you and set out straightaway. She should arrive there shortly."

His smile broadened. "Thank you very much! I'll keep an eye out for her."

"Good. You take good care of her, alright?" The girl's voice grew stern.

"I will. I promise," North spoke without hesitation.

A short while later, he caught sight of a figure coming over the hill. Her long white winter coat blended in with the snowy scene, but he would recognize her anywhere. North admired the way Cascadia's coat hugged her ample curves, the way her dark waves cascaded from her fur-trimmed hood.

Determination powered her every step, not an ounce of uncertainty in her entire being. When, at last, she reached the front of the bed and breakfast, North hurried to get the door for her. He took her coat and hung it as she shook the snowflakes out of her hair, her smile soft.

Beneath it, she wore a powder-blue sweater with a snowflake pattern. The way it clung to her hips and wrapped around her body made North warm with desire. Cascadia looked absolutely breathtaking in the knitted dress, her dark hair falling over her shoulders. He reached for her then, wrapping her in a warm embrace.

As his selkie returned the hug, North thought that he might melt like Frosty the Snowman right then and there. Completely content and in love.

"You have news?" she asked softly, pulling away just slightly.

"Yes! The most wonderful, magical news." North took her hands in his. "Ms. Eve has offered me a job managing the bed and breakfast. I'm staying in Seaside. With you, I hope."

Those deep, observant eyes roved his face for several long seconds. North held his breath. Then Cascadia threw her arms around his neck, stretching up on her tiptoes to kiss his cheek. The temptation to kiss her senseless, to wrap his hands over her supple hips and pull her to him, nearly undid him.

But the elf managed, just barely, to restrain himself for the moment.

"Are you...will you go back to the sea?" North whispered the question into her ear.

"No. No sea. I must stay here. There is work to do," Cascadia murmured into his neck. "I will stay with Emmy and Marissa, and we will help our kin survive."

He took a deep, steadying breath. "You want to stay on land? And give up everything you've known for this?"

"I can do more good from land, for my pod. I can stay with you." Her breath tickled his cheek.

His lips were upon her in an instant. North wrapped both arms around her back, pulling his selkie flush against him. Her lips were just as insistent as they gasped and nipped and explored each others' mouths. When she tangled one hand in his blonde locks and tugged lightly, North took in a sharp breath.

Cascadia tasted like dark, rich chocolate. Sweet with just a hint of bitterness lingering at the back. Like hot cocoa with a pinch of cayenne pepper to give it a kick. He knew, from that day forward, the rest of his life would be the same—not a moment of boredom or predictability.

An adventure with his dark-eyed selkie, full of twists and turns and unexpected changes. North could think of nothing he wanted more in the whole world than this.

Epilogue

CASCADIA

One Year Later

The day before Christmas arrived in a flurry of snow. Fluffy white clouds lined the sky and dropped snowflakes on land and sea indiscriminately. Frost coated the windowpanes of the North Pole Bed and Breakfast as Cascadia crawled out of bed just before six in the morning. Her night had consisted of mostly tossing and turning, so she had decided to simply start her day.

Soft, fuzzy slippers and a pair of fleece pajamas felt nearly as good against her skin as her fur had when she was in her seal form. Her feet made little tapping sounds as she crossed the room and slipped out into the foyer. It took only a moment to turn on the roaring fire in the brick fireplace of the front room, then she settled in the cozy green armchair.

Cascadia's thoughts danced a slow ballet through her mind as she reflected on the past year. Her first year on land; her first year with North. In that time, this place had become her home just as much as the half-submerged caves where she had grown up with her sisters.

A little jingle sounded as Ms. Eve slipped into the room, her festive earrings bouncing with each step. The little old lady carried a wooden tray in both hands, setting it carefully upon the wooden coffee table before the fire. Cascadia smiled warmly at the elf.

"Good morning, my dear," said Ms. Eve cheerily. "I thought you might want something to munch on this morning."

"Good morning."

She accepted the red Santa mug filled nearly to the top with steaming cocoa. A little peppermint spoon melted slowly into the chocolate as Cascadia swirled it around. On the tray, she found a little loaf of fresh baked coffee cake—the kind with the almond filling and vanilla glaze. Her favorite.

Ever since she had first tried it, Ms. Eve had made a point of surprising her with the treat at regular intervals. The selkie was still adjusting to being doted on by everyone: Emmy and her gran, Ms. Eve, North, and even David at the coffee shop. Since they had found out she and North were expecting their first child, there had been no stopping the others from fussing.

This evening, North's family would arrive from the North Pole for the first time to meet her and see Oregon. They had been quite hesitant at first about leaving the safety of home, being able to fit in among the humans for even a short period of time. But eventually the longing to see him had been enough to convince them to make a short trip.

Until then, all Cascadia needed to do was rest. Her

maternity leave had started last week and she intended to make the most of this time off with her husband. They had married in March, only a few months after she had come to land for the very first time.

A small, quiet winter wedding on the snowy beach, followed by months of married bliss. She adored falling asleep wrapped in North's strong arms and waking up each morning snuggled up against his warm body. The family they had cobbled together in Seaside over those months felt just as important to her as the pod she'd left behind.

"I know it's too much sugar first thing in the morning," Ms. Eve said grumpily. "But we'll have a proper bacon and eggs breakfast after that lazybones husband of yours wakes up, hmm?"

Cascadia giggled uncontrollably at that. "Sleeping in until nearly seven thirty! How luxurious."

"Some of us have work to do," grumbled the older woman.

But the truth remained: Ms. Eve took the early shift, managing the stock room and the kitchen, while North handled most of the day-to-day guest work. She would slip away around four in the afternoon, to have a little nap in her room like a cat sleeping in a sunbeam. Then the three of them and any guests currently staying at the bed and breakfast would have dinner.

Dessert always capped off the meal, something decadent and homemade that the older woman had made in the wee hours of the morning. For Cascadia, the hum of their rhythm around the house felt as soothing as the sound of the waves crashing on the beach. Their little home beside the sea was full of love and joy.

She knew her daughter would grow up surrounded by this community, a selkie in name only, part of the local lore. When she arrived, Cascadia would spend six months at home caring for her while doing part time consulting work for conservation nonprofits. Her efforts to study the human world and learn how it interacted with the seas had paid off substantially.

Word had spread of the pretty young woman with an uncanny ability to understand the sea creatures and the needs of the ocean in ways no one quite understood. Cascadia loved her full time job at Oregon Shores, where she led dozens of monthly beach clean-ups in between her usual efforts to repair the oceans. All year, she had made small suggestions and changes to the way things were done that improved the health of the sea.

The front door to the bed and breakfast opened, revealing her red-headed cousin Emmy and her sister, Ellery. Matching grins lit their faces as they slipped out of their winter gear and hurried over to her.

"Sister! I have met the most wonderful girl," Ellery exclaimed.

"Oh?" Cascadia asked, glancing at her cousin.

"Her hair is the color of the sky when the sun goes down," continued her sister excitedly. "Her name is Addison and I have a date this afternoon!"

The three young ladies sat together, chatting and eating the coffee cake for hours while they warmed themselves by the fire. It had never occurred to Cascadia that a selkie might fall in love with a woman—they came to land to get pregnant and secure the future of their pod. Yet the light in her sister's eyes made her think of the way she had felt after that first date with North.

Perhaps this would mean that Ellery would stay on land with a human lover, and be nearby while Cascadia's daughter grew up. The thought made her heart ache with happiness. To have her family surrounding her like that would be a Christmas miracle. Much like finding her elf in the midst of her early days on land and falling head over fins for him instantly.

Morning turned to evening with little fuss around the North Pole Bed and Breakfast. Ms. Eve disappeared at the usual time for her afternoon nap and North answered the phones. The couple staying in Room B came back just before dinner, holding hands and gazing at each other all starry-eyed. A selkie called Lunaria had arrived on land a few weeks ago and Emmy had had no trouble finding a young man to her liking.

As she and Emmy cleared the plates, the front door opened once more. In stepped a short man with blonde hair going white around the temples and a woman just a bit shorter still. Her blonde hair and bright blue eyes were immediately recognizable. Behind them, another elf clomped into the room and knocked the snow off his boots.

"You made it!" North cried. "Welcome to our happy little home."

"Yes, well, that magical sleigh ride was certainly something, wasn't it?" his father called back in a cheerful tone as he hung their coats.

"Isn't it spectacular?" North grinned broadly.

It made Cascadia smile. He still spoke of his crossing the ocean and seeing humpback whales close enough to get splashed. North's journey had brought him to her, and now his family had braved the trip to visit them.

"I think the penguins were my favorite part," said his mother, wrapping him in a tight hug.

"Mama, Papa, I'd like you to meet my wife, Cascadia," said North, pride and joy in his voice. "She has stolen my heart quite completely and I've never been happier."

Both of his parents wrapped her in their arms, murmuring kind words. "I am so happy you all made it safely to Oregon, despite the chilly weather."

"Well, she's even prettier in person, snowflake," said West, winking at Cascadia. "Here's to hoping your little one takes after her!"

North playfully punched his brother in the shoulder and the two bickered back and forth for several moments. She liked the way it felt, their parents looking on with fond smiles and the brothers teasing each other. When they finally settled, Ms. Eve stepped up beside Cascadia and introduced herself.

Though she knew the older woman had lived in Seaside for many decades, the Snowstorm family greeted her like an old friend. It seemed all Christmas elves were the jovial, welcoming sort. Knowing that her daughter would grow up amongst that kind of warmth made Cascadia unbelievably happy.

"This is my sister, Ellery," she spoke up, gesturing the selkie forward.

"How lovely! I do hope you're enjoying your time on land, my dear," Mrs. Snowstorm said.

"And my cousin, Emmy," Cascadia added as the red-headed girl stepped into the circle.

"Enchanted to meet you," West said, kissing Emmy's hand. "I see beauty runs in the family."

The blush that spread across her cousin's cheeks at that flirty compliment nearly matched the red Christmas sweater she wore. Her bright eyes took in every inch of the handsome elf and Cascadia couldn't help but laugh. She had had nearly the same reaction to North when they had met, so she understood the appeal all too well.

Soon, everyone was settled in front of the fire, chatting in little groups. Ms. Eve brought out steamy cups of hot chocolate for everyone and a selection of home-made Christmas cookies. It didn't take long for the sweets to disappear, delicious as they were.

Cascadia made a mental note to write down all of the older woman's recipes after Christmas. Without a doubt, the North Pole Bed and Breakfast would keep using those recipes for generations. A yawn overtook her then and her doting husband turned to her.

"Do you need to go to bed, my love?"

"I am afraid so," Cascadia whispered sleepily. "Goodnight, my family and friends."

Hugs were given all around, then North wrapped one strong arm around her waist and guided her to their room. He helped her change into her pajamas and kissed her round belly as she pulled on the shirt, his blue eyes misty.

"I love our little life here. Our family," her elf murmured against her forehead as she snuggled up against him.

"Me, too, North. I love you."

THE END.

. . .

Acknowledgments

This book has been a wonderful journey for me, made possible by some lovely indie author friends I've made this year. The AZ Authors girlies, thank you for adopting me into your midst despite my living in Texas. Your friendship, support, encouragement, and mentorship this year have absolutely changed the trajectory of my writing career.

You've added so much joy to my life with your group chats and shenanigans! From Kickstarter to author events to collaborations like this, I've found myself challenged and championed left and right by my girls. Here's to the first of many group writing projects over the coming years and endless trips to Phoenix!

All year, I've learned and grown and written at new levels because of you. You've taught me so much and kept me on my toes. If someone had told me in January of this year that I would be releasing two holiday romances in the month of November, I would have said they're insane. And two Kickstarter campaigns. And now, with ten author events under my belt, I feel confident stepping into my future with these new skills.

I'm sure I've taken on entirely too many events for next year, and too many writing projects! I'm sure it will push me to my limits a few times. But I also know that I adore facing the wild west that is indie authorship with such a wonderful group of friends by my side. A community of like-minded women who continue to make magic for the world in these devastating times, when we so desperately need it.

Thank you to my indie author friends. Thank you to the AZ Authors group. Thank you to all the friends I've made along the way on this writing journey so far.

About the Author

Kay Leyda grew up in the Chicago suburbs in the 90s and 00s, an avid reader who spent many weekends in her local library consuming as many books as she could get her hands on.

She moved to Florida in her early twenties, where she spent several years working at Walt Disney World and enjoying life in Orlando. She has been writing and storytelling all her life.

After getting her associate's degree at Valencia College in Orlando, she relocated to the Florida Panhandle to focus on completing her Bachelor of Clinical Psychology from the University of Central Florida.

During the early days of the pandemic, she began drafting what would eventually become the first Piscea book. In 2021, she turned 30, graduated from UCF, and married the love of her life.

Currently she spends her days baking, listening to romantic comedies, and daydreaming up new love stories to tell the world.

[illegible]

[illegible]

After graduating, her associate degree [illegible] College in Orlando, she relocated [illegible] Florida [illegible] completing her Bachelor of Clinical Psychology from the University of Central Florida.

During the early [illegible] of the pandemic, [illegible] would eventually become the first [illegible]

Currently, she [illegible] days [illegible] to [illegible] to the public.

Where to Find Kay Leyda

Where to find Kay Leyda

Instagram: https://www.instagram.com/kayleydaauthor/?hl=en

Facebook: https://www.facebook.com/KayEskewAuthor/

Threads: https://www.threads.com/@kayleydaauthor

Tiktok: https://www.tiktok.com/@kayleydaauthor

BookBub: https://www.bookbub.com/profile/kay-leyda

Beventi: https://beventi.co/author/kayleydaauthor0

Author Website: https://kayleydaauthor.com/

Signed Copies: https://beventi.co/orderform/0udbnsrj5c

Where to find Kay Leyda's books

Amazon: https://www.amazon.com/stores/Kay-Leyda/author/B0CSBYLJZR

Barnes & Noble: https://www.barnesandnoble.com/s/%22Kay%20Leyda

Goodreads: https://www.goodreads.com/author/list/47877027.Kay_Leyda

Also by Kay Leyda

The Piscea Chronicles – A Young Adult Fantasy Trilogy for teens

Of Seafoam & Saltwater (Book 1)

Of Magic & Moonlight (Book 2)

Of Depths & Darkness (Book 3) (Coming soon!)

Winter Wonderland Amusement Park – Closed-door Holiday Romcoms for Hallmark lovers

Under Sparkling Lights (Book 1)

Mrs. Claus's Confectionary (Book 1.5 – short story)

TITLE TO BE ANNOUNCED (Book 2) (Coming out in late 2026)

Standalone Books

Seashells & Mistletoe – A Holiday Novella, part of the Blue Christmas Collective

TITLE TO BE ANNOUNCED - Secret Garden short story retelling, part of the Flipped Fairytales Series

Cozy Christmas Collective

Cocoa & Clauses by Ava Fleur

Cookies & Claws by Fleur DeVillainy

Sugar & Snowflakes by Kristin Cast

Seashells & Mistletoe by Kay Leyda

Made in the USA
Coppell, TX
08 December 2025